THE BERRY HOUSE

FREE IMAGINATION

F/I

ATLANTA

EARL FREEMAN

THE BERRY HOUSE

FREE IMAGINATION

F/I

ATLANTA

The library of congress cataloging-in-publication data is available upon request

Free Imagination ISBN: 978-0-692-76078-9

Book cover illustrated by Xavier Mclendon

www.freeimaginationpublishing.com

Printed in the United States of America

This book is dedicated to my beautiful wife Kelly Freeman. Thank you for loving me, when there was nothing to love, but me.

I Thank God for my wonderful children, Tieara, Ronald, Evion and Markel.

EARL FREEMAN AND DEANETTE
ATKINFEST

My father and mother

Thank you for life

Daddy, I want to take this time to thank you, for all the love you gave to me and my brother's. You were a single father, who always took the time to spend with us. You always made me feel loved and wanted. You showed me how to be a man. I love you daddy and I am thankful for you. Thanks for being my father.

I love you,

Earl Freeman

Your proud son

To all my family members. If I held a pen, you all were the ink. I thank you all for all the love and support.

To all my uncles and aunts, you all shaped me into the person I am.

To all my friends and supporters, thank you all and much love.

To my brothers, Gerald and Lamont, we got us one.

"THE GREATEST DISCOVERY OF ALL MANKIND IS THE DISCOVERY OF SELF."

EARL FREEMAN

WELCOME INTO THE MIND OF

EARL FREEMAN

THE BERRY HOUSE

CHAPTER 1

THE CHASE

On a beautiful hot Georgia day, Bobby Berry is just getting out of school and is ready to take a long walk home. He is 12 years old and is in the 7th grade. He is a straight A student and has lots of friends. This is a walk he dreads.

He says bye, to his classmates and begins to walk home. He sees' his mother's car pulling into the school's parking lot. He is surprised, but happy to see his mother coming to pick him up.

He runs over to the car as fast as he can, with a big smile of appreciation on his face. He's sure this is his mother's car, because it's a black Mercedes Benz with extra dark tented windows. The windows are so dark that, you can't see inside. He was sure it was her.

Bobby opened the car door on the passenger side and started to put on his seat belt. "Hey mom!" he said, with cheer and relief, that he didn't have to walk home. Then suddenly, a look of confusion spread across his face, "why are you driving mama's car?" Bobby asked, his older brother Anthony.

"Mama told me to pick you up today," he says, as he peels out the parking lot like a bat out of hell. Bobby's head hits the back of his seat, from the power of the car's acceleration.

Anthony is 3 years older than Bobby. He is 15 years old and is always in some kind of trouble.

"I know you're lying! Mama didn't let you drive nowhere! You don't even have a driver's license yet! Let me out of this car! I want to call mama!" Bobby says, in an angry voice, hoping that his brother would slow down, so he can get out the speeding car.

"Man shut up! We going home!"

"You took mama's car!" Bobby says, as Anthony continued to drive crazy through the streets.

Anthony did not reply. He was too busy trying to concentrate, while driving reckless. "Where is mama?" Young Bobby asked, in a shaking voice.

"She gone! Stop asking so many fucking questions shawty. Damn! Just shut up." Anthony fires back in a very rude tone, as he clinches his fist, as if he was about to knock the fire out his younger brother. Scared, Bobby suddenly gets quite. He holds on to his seat and just hopes his crazy brother doesn't crash.

Anthony continued to drive like a bat straight out of hell, weaving in and out of traffic like a mad man. He was running every stop sign and red light. All the while, Bobby is scared and holding on for dear life. His heart is beating over 100 beats per second. He is begging and pleading to his brother to stop, slow down and let him out of the car. Bobby doesn't want to have anything to do with this wild roller coaster ride.

Then, all the sudden out of nowhere, come two police cars with lights wailing and sirens roaring, coming up fast behind Anthony. The next thing you know he panics and floors it, doing speeds up to 65 mph in a residential zone. Cars begin to pull off to the side of the road, as Anthony pass by terrorizing the community with his reckless driving.

"We going to jail!" Bobby yells out at the top of his voice. Anthony is now sweating profusely, looking over his shoulder.

"Fuck them muthafuckas. I ain't going nowhere," he says, as he braces himself, locking his elbows and hands on the steering wheel of his mom's car.

Then suddenly, another cop car joins in on the chase for back up. Now there are three cop cars chasing him. Anthony is really nervous and sweating, this has now gone from bad to worse.

"I got to shake these muthafuckas!" he says, as he looks into his rear-view mirror.

"Pull over your vehicle now! Pull over the vehicle right now!" the officer yells from the speaker, in a demanding voice, driving directly behind Anthony. Bobby is screaming and holding on for dear life, as if he was on a roller coaster. His feet pressed against the floor board, as if he was pressing the breaks. He nervously looks around, as everything is moving at the speed of light. To him, he sees his life falling apart.

To Bobby things seemed to be moving in slow motion, somewhat unreal. He was thinking to himself, this is like a scene from a movie. A nightmare.

"Slow down!!!" Bobby yells out again.

"Fuck that! They gone have to catch me," Anthony replies, looking over his right shoulder.

Then, he increased his speed by 30 mph. The motor roared like a lion. So, he's now doing about 90 mph in a neighborhood full of kids. They are unaware of the terror that lies ahead. As Anthony watched the three cop cars hot on his tail, he continues looking through his rear view mirror and looking over his shoulder. He was not an experienced driver and he was going too fast and was not paying any attention to where he was driving. He did not see the two little girls playing near the street. He went speeding uncontrollably around the corner.

"Watch out Anthony!" Bobby yelled, as Anthony turned into the cross intersection. Bobby puts up both his arms to cover his head, as he sank into the seat of the speeding car. The next thing you know, there is the sound of screeching tires and screaming kids. Smoke is billowing in the air. The smell of rubber is strong. Anthony suddenly hits the breaks. For a moment, there is total silence. The cops pull back and the chase is over.

CHAPTER 2

THE AFTERMATH

Bobby squints his eyes, as he wakes up from being unconscious for the last past two days. As he tries to open his eyes and focus, he noticed that his hand is cuffed to a hospital bed.

"Where am I?" Bobby asked, with blurred vision looking around the room. "And why I am hand cuffed to this bed?" he adds, in a weak voice.

"You're waking up," the nurse says, as she tucked the sheets underneath Bobby.

"Just hold on, I will get your mother," the nurse says as she exits the room looking back at him. Then Bobby looks over to his right and sees an officer sitting in a chair with his eyes closed, head leaning forward and drool falling from his mouth. It appeared that the officer is having a nap while on duty.

"What's going on sir? What happened to me?" Bobby asked.

He doesn't remember anything about what happened two days before. He has suffered a severe head and neck injuries from the car crash.

"Well," the officer says, as he walks over to Bobby's bed pulling up his utility belt and wiping his mouth. "Son, it's not looking good for you right now. Your brother is in the juvenile detention center facing DMV and vehicle manslaughter."

Bobby's brown eyes grew big. He looked surprised, while taking a big gulp. His throat was as dry as an Arizona desert.

"What does that mean?" Bobby asked the officer.

"Well, son, to make a long story short, you and your brother done got y'all self in some deep shit. Your brother is charged with murder by a vehicle and stealing a car and you... you an accessory to the crime. That means, they think you helped him." Then he paused.

"Two days ago your bother hit and killed a six year old little girl, while y'all was running from the law."

Bobby's small frame flopped backwards in his hospital bed. Then suddenly, the events start to come back to him. There is a pause. He lays in disbelief. "But I didn't even do anything. I remember now... I can remember everything now."

Bobby continued staring into the distance. "My brother stole my mama's car and came to pick me up from school."

"Why did you get in the car with him?" he asked, with a yeah right smirk on his face.

"Because my mama has real dark tented windows on her car and you can't see on the inside. I thought it was my mama coming to pick me up from school."

"Bobby, thank God you're ok," Bobby's mother said, excitedly as she entered into the room putting her forgiving loving arms around her youngest son.

"Mom!" Bobby says, with excitement. His eyes lit up, as he watched his mother enter the room. "I'm so glad to see you," he added hugging his mother with one free arm.

Bobby held on tight to his mother. "Mama, where is my brother?"

"Well, he's in the Berry House," his mother replied, with a heavy heart.

The Berry House is a slang name for the local juvenile detention center.

"Is he okay?" Bobby asked, concerned about his older, but trouble brother.

"Yes. He is going to be just fine. I talked to him earlier today. He's okay. It's you um worried about," she says, forcing a smile upon her worried face. "How is mama's big boy?"

"I'm okay. I'm glad you are here with me," Bobby replied, with a worried look in eyes. "Can you stay here with me? I'm scared mama."

Bobby begins to cry, as he apologizes and tells his mother about the horrible events that unfolded just days before. He told his mother all about how Anthony had stolen the car and came to the school to pick him up. He explained how he thought it was her driving. Then, he told her about how Anthony was driving recklessly through the neighborhood, scaring everyone. He even told her how Anthony tried to out run the police and how he had a big crash. Apparently, Bobby didn't realize that a little girl had been hit and killed during the high speed chase.

Bobby's mother rubbed his head, as he sobbed uncontrollable. "Bobby-Bobby, it's going to be okay baby. I promise," she says, as she tries to comfort him and stop him from crying.

"I'm innocent mama. I didn't hurt anybody. I didn't kill anybody," he said, looking up at his mother. "I was getting ready to walk home from school. Why did this have to happen to me mama? Why?" Bobby asked, as the tears flowed from his eyes, and down his cheeks.

"I know...I know baby. I talked to your brother and he told me the truth. He told me everything. I already know that you didn't have anything to do with this mess." He listened closely, as his mother continued to speak. "I know Anthony took my car and he told me, you didn't have anything to do with it. You gone be okay."

Bobby had an expression on his face, like the weight of the world has been lifted off his back. "So, Bobby you are going to be just fine. Just hang in there for mama," she added, as she held him tight.

"Does that mean I get to go home, when I get out the hospital?" Bobby asked, in a calm innocent voice.

She had to tell him the sad news, "you still have to go to the juvenile detention center, even though you weren't driving." She struggled to be strong for him. She held back the tears from rolling down her face. Finally, she broke down, as she explained, the whole innocent until proven guilty thing.

He was trying to be strong for his crying mother, telling her not to cry and he was going to be okay. Now, their roles have reversed. He grabbed a napkin, that's sitting on the table next to the bed. He began wiping his mother's face, asking her to stop crying.

Just then, the nurse informed Ms. Berry, that her visit was now over. Bobby's mother turned to the nurse and asked for just five more minutes, which was granted. His mother encouraged him to be good and told everything was going to be just fine. Then, his mother gave him a hug and a big kiss.

"Okay Ms. Berry, you have to say good night to Bobby." The nurse called from behind her again saying, "it's time to say good night," indicating that her visit was now over.

Before she exited the room, she turned to Officer Hall and said, "sir, don't let nothing happen to my baby."

"Yes ma'am... I'll make sure I watch over him," he replied, as she exited out the door.

The next day, Bobby is cleared by the medical staff to be released to his mother, but because of pending charges he was escorted from the hospital straight to Earl Freeman JDC. JDC is an acronym for Juvenile Detention Center. This is where youthful juvenile offenders are held until they are sentenced or go home.

The nurse came to Bobby's bed side and told him that he is being released from the hospital. There was a strange man with her. The man was dressed in a juvenile detention Officer's uniform. He had hand restraints in one hand and legs shackles in the other hand. When Bobby saw the man with the hand cuffs and leg irons, he took a deep breath, as if it was his last breath of life. Right then and there, things just got real. He figured it was his last breath of freedom, as he knew it.

"Bobby, my name is Officer Hill." Then the officer went on to say, "um the transporting officer at Freeman JDC. You will be coming with me.

This man spoke with a heavy southern accent. He looked like the type of guy that would be sitting in front of a store, hanging out with his buddies all day, cutting on something with his pocket knife. One of them good ole country boys. He looks like the type that just might call you a nigger, as you walked by. Overalls, big belly and all. Oh yeah, don't forget about the reading glasses and the chewing tobacco in his cheeks.

"Am I going to jail?" Bobby asked, the southern officer.

"Well, technically it's not jail. It's a juvenile detention center," he replied.

The officer gave Bobby a size medium beige jumpsuit, and uncuffed him from the bed and told him to put on the county jail jumpsuit. He reluctantly did just as the officer ordered and put on the old dingy uniform. He placed the handcuffs and leg irons on him and escorted him out of the hospital, into his county patrol car. During the long drive, all he could think of was, why did this have to happen to him? After all, he was a good kid, who has never been in any kind of trouble at all. He was also a straight A student with

BIG dreams. He couldn't believe this was really happening to him. This was like a bad dream of some sort, but unfortunately for him, this was not a bad dream. In fact, it was reality. Bobby Berry's reality. As the officer talked to him, his mind drifted back to the roller coaster ride with his brother Anthony.

He thought about all the horror stories he had heard about the Berry House. The more he thought about the things he had heard, the more he became sick to his stomach. The more frighten he became and the more he blocked out officer Hill.

All he ever heard about the Berry house was, how there was always bullying, fighting and someone trying to get your booty. Who wouldn't be scared?

This seemed to be the longest trip ever for him. After about 57 minutes or so of driving, Officer Hill and Bobby arrived at the detention center. The location of the facility was in the middle of nowhere. Literally, nothing was around nor close by. There were no stores. Nothing. Just a big old run down building.

Just looking at the building, you just knew, this was no place where you wanted to be, not even for a minute. The building rests on the top of a twenty feet hill. This made it hard to gain access to and from the facility. The building was very gloomy and scary looking. Just looking at the building, gave him the creeps and the chills.

The building was gray and was surrounded by a 20 feet high fence with sharp razor wire at the top. Trust me, from the looks of things, nobody was escaping out this place alive. All around the fence was signs with big bold, red and white letters that read, "Warning razor sharp- DO NOT TOUCH!"

There were other signs that read, "Warning- DO NOT ATTEMPT TO CROSS THIS LINE."

He takes a big gulp, as he looked around. Needless to say, he didn't like what he saw. The closer the officer and he got, the more nervous he became.

By now, um sure you guessed it, poor Bobby is shaking like a leaf on a tree, in the   dead of winter time.

"This place looks very scary," he says, in a whisper like tone, as the officer pulled up the steep hill into the facility parking lot.

"Is this where um coming?" he asked, in a low voice.

"Yes, this here is your destination... this is Earl Freeman JDC," Officer Hill answered.

"Is this place as bad as they say it is?" Bobby asked, with fright in his voice.

"No, It's really that bad. The kids do like to fight a lot from time to time, but if anybody mess with you, just tell an officer and they will look after you. Don't worry too much. You will be just fine," Officer Hill says, glancing back at him through his review mirror.

"Yes sir," Bobby replied looking out the window.

The juvenile detention center was an all-male 70 bed facility at its full capacity. On the male unit, there was a dayroom and three halls, which where B, C, and D. A hall was once for the females, before the detention center become an all-male center some years ago. Just outside the unit, there was the central control room. This room held all the control boards, that operated the whole facility. The multi-purpose area was located just in front of central control, which led into the dining area and the kitchen. Also on site was the administration department, a recreation yard, as well as two trailers, that were used for the education department.

CHAPTER 3

INTAKE

"Please state your name and the nature of your business," a voice calls out over the small speaker just outside the intake door.

"Yes, ma'am this is Officer Hill with transportation. I have one new male juvenile for intake processing," calls out Officer Hill, as he spits what seemed like an 8 ounces of tobacco on the ground outside. Then there's a loud buzzing sound, as the sally port door opens.

Once inside, the intake process begins. Officer Hill took the cuffs off Bobby. He signs a hand full of papers and tells him good luck and he was gone.

Bobby is taken into a small room stripped searched (all cloths are removed from head to toe). He already feels violated and humiliated. He hated this place already. The intake officer gave him a set of underwear, which look like his daddy may have worn them back in the day. He was also given some socks, pants, t-shirts, shower shoes and gym shoes which were two sizes too big.

After getting dressed, he was directed to sit down and he was asked a series of questions, kind of like an interview session. During the intake interview the intake officer asked him did he and his brother kill someone? Bobby tried explaining the situation, but the intake officer wasn't interested in what he had to say. The officer didn't tell him his name, not one time.

It seemed like the intake officer already had Bobby and his brother guilty without a trial. From that, he already knew this was going to be a long, long ride, one that he would rather not take.

 After forty-five minutes of question after question, he was done with the intake process.

"What are we going to do now?" he asked nervously.

"Next, you will shower. Then after that you will be going to the unit," he explained. Then the officer gathered his clothes and shoes. Bobby entered the shower.

 Once he took his shower, the intake officer and he walked to the unit. This seemed to be the longest walk he has ever taken in his life. They could hear the chaos before they made it to the unit door. The stench of the unit hit his nose like a knockout punch. The smell was horrific turning his stomach upside down. He almost threw up, causing him to clutch his mouth. There was the sound of kids and officers yelling. This really made him nervous.

"Y'all need to sit y'all bad asses down somewhere!" Officer Simms says, at the top of his voice, "get on my damn nerves!" he added, with obvious frustration.

"Shut yo gay ass up!" a voice called out from the back of the dayroom.

"Yo bald head ass granny," Officer Simms fires back, as he watches the uncontrollable residents run around wild. He has his hands on his hips with his lips poked out, shining like brand new chrome. He looked in the direction from where the insults came from, trying to see who made the disrespectful comment about him.

Officer Simms has been a juvenile corrections officer for five years. He is very flamboyant and colorful. Officer Simms stands about 6'2" and is a little on the heavy side. The residents always give him a hard time, but they all love him. He is also a great officer and doesn't take no mess from nobody. Period.

Soon, the other officer's join in to assist Officer Simms to gain control of the unit. Bobby could not believe what his eyes where seeing. This was like something straight out of the movies. The unit was totally out of control. There were about 45 boys and most of them were running wild, rapping and yelling really loud.

"Officer Hill (not to be confused with the transportation Officer), go get that damn camera. Um bout to shut this muthafucka down. Um tired of this shit," said Officer Simms looking across the dayroom.

"Okay- I'll be right back," Officer Hill replied.

Officer Hill ran to the control room and yells, "Give me the camera!"

With camera in hand, he begins filming the incidents. When the residents see Officer Hill filming them, they all begin to run to their rooms to avoid being wrote up and being put on lockdown, for not complying with the officer's commands. After a lot of screaming, chasing and yelling, the officers begin to gain control and securing the residents in their rooms.

"Who is that? Where did he come from?" Officer Parker asks the intake officer looking at Bobby. After locking down all the others kids, he is still breathing hard from chasing the residents up and down the hall. He bends over to catch his breath. He puts his hands on his knees. Officer Parker is about 5'8". He is brown complexion and has a bald head. He was in the marines. So, you already know he didn't joke with the residents. He didn't play the radio. This dude never smiled. He stayed with an attitude.

"This is Bobby Berry," the intake officer replied.

"Well lock his ass down too," said Officer Parker with a frown on his face.

"These damn kids done lost their minds. We had to lock this bitch down," Officer Simms said, as he gently wipes sweat from his face and takes a deep breath. "Shit!" he adds.

Bobby is sitting there looking dumb founded. This was some introduction for him. This place was like a zoo, to say least.

He was in shock and he knew it was going to be a long ride. The first impression was an ever lasting impression on his mind and it was not a good one to remember. He had heard so many things about the Berry House. Now, he sees it for himself. It was wild and crazy. He had been on the unit only about ten minutes, and he hated it already. He just got to the place and it was already on lock down.

That night, Bobby tosses and turns all night long. He could not sleep at all. He kept thinking, this place was just like a zoo. The other residents stayed up all night rapping, banging, yelling and kicking on their doors. On top of that, the officer was doing rounds all night, which meant they were putting the flash light in his face every thirty minutes. He cried himself to sleep that night. He could not believe that this was really happening to him. This was the worst night of his whole life. And it was only his first day.

This was a living nightmare. All he could think about was going through all this for nothing. All this, just because his stupid brother decided to steal his mom's car and go on a joy ride.

CHAPTER 4

GENERAL POP

The next day started like the previous night ended-chaotic!

"Breakfast time, breakfast time, wake up," the officer's yelled as they walked up and down the unit, banging on the doors with the butts of their flash lights. Bobby woke up looking as if he had a bad dream. He felt as though he had been hit by a mac truck. The residents were given 15 minutes to get prepared for breakfast. Then they were lined up and escorted to the dining area for Sunday morning breakfast.

The breakfast looked gross. The eggs ran like a track star. The biscuits, well one boy hide one underneath his shirt; it was hard enough to use as a jail house weapon. And the oat meal was trying to catch up with the eggs. Bobby didn't touch a thing on his tray; however, the others residents, well you would have thought they was at Golden Corral or somewhere. They were tearing that nasty food up.

After the breakfast was complete the kids had church service in the dining area. Yelp, that's right. They had church in the juvenile center too. What did you think, they didn't have church just because they were locked up? Wrong.

The preacher on this morning talked about "freedom." He walked in dressed very nice. The man wore a three piece suit. He was a short black man in statue. He is about 5'4" and sported a bald head. He looked to be in his mid-30s. He had two other gentlemen with him, but the other two didn't say much the whole time.

The preacher was short indeed, but the man still stood tall.

"Freedom!" the preacher said, loud and abrupt. "Freedom is a beautiful thing. Do any of you all know what freedom is?" he paused for a moment, looking at the boys, as if he was waiting on a response. Then he proceeded. "How many of you all know freedom is not free? I remember being in a place like this, when I was young just like you. I never appreciated how much it meant to be free, until they took my freedom away from me. I never thought nothing about being free at all, until I got my butt locked up."

Then, he went on to say, "most of you didn't appreciate your freedom until it was snatched away.

Listen young boys, I didn't become free until I got locked up."

They all had a look on their faces, as if they were lost or dumbfounded. But you could tell the ones that were paying attention and the ones who didn't gave a care.

"That's right," he says.

"I was locked up when I was free. I didn't know it or realize it. I didn't become free until I got locked up. Right now, most of you all are double locked up. I'm going tell you all what um talking about in a minute," the man says wiping his mouth with a red handkerchief, as he pauses.

"Don't none of you all want to hear nothing about no freedom. You all think um talking crazy up in here. You all don't want to be free."

"I want to be free," a small voice calls out quietly from the back.

"Who said that?" he asks, as he looks up.

"I did," said a boy, sitting in the back of the dining room.

"Tell them again," said the preacher.

"I want to be free," he said, but this time in a much louder voice.

"That's what um talking about!" in an almost shouting tone, the preacher gets excited. He went on to say, "I wasn't free at all. I was a slave to gang banging and cane slanging. I was a slave to drugs, alcohol and women. Anything that was thuggish, I was doing it. I was a slave. Here I was thinking just because I was free, I thought I was free, on the streets. When in reality, I wasn't free at all. I was locked up by the chains of my mind, and I didn't even know it."

The preacher paused again, then he began to speak in a louder tone of voice saying, "when I got locked up, I started to see a lot of things. My vision became 20/20. It wasn't until I was locked up, when I realized that I really wasn't free at all. All the homeboys I thought I had, none of them accepted my phone calls when I got locked up. Not one, of my so called friends, ever wrote me back. None of my boys even tried to come and see me. I started to realize, all these friends I thought I had, really wasn't my friends at all. There were people around to use me, misguide me and misdirect me. To this day, you know where most of them are?" he asked and the room was silent, as he paused.

"Most of them are dead and the others are locked up. That's right, locked up. This is what um trying to tell you all. God loved me enough to lock me up, so he could give me freedom. Anybody want to be free today? Raise your hand."

The group of young boys, all quietly raised their hands. The preacher paused and slowly looked around the room. By their reaction, he knew he had their attention. Then he continued.

"No... I'm not talking about going home and being free. No that's short lived freedom. If you don't change, you gone come right back in here anyway. So, um not talking about going home. It's way bigger than that. Um talking about being free mentally and spiritually, so you can be free physically. You all know the devil is mad now. See, he doesn't like it when you all get information like this. See, the devil doesn't mind you all watching BET and MTV, all day long. See, he doesn't mind ya'll talking about robbing and killing folks. He mad now!!!!! But that's all right, cause um gone keep on preaching."

"Preach it!" an officer said, from the back of the room.

The preacher's voice rose once more. "I'm talking about freedom, the kind of freedom where you can be free, no matter if you're locked up or locked down. I'm talking about freedom in your mind, freedom in your spirit and freedom in your soul. Nobody can take that from you. I'm talking about real freedom. Don't you want it?" he said, in a lower tone of voice, as he wipes sweat off of his face.

"I know a whole lot of rich people, who wish they had the freedom um talking about. I know a lot of famous movie stars who would give it all away just to have freedom. And you know what, it don't cost a dime. Um here to tell y'all, you can be as free as you want to be. If only you believe in the father and the son. I'm talking about the Lord Jesus Christ, our Lord and Savior," then the preacher takes out his handkerchief and wipes the sweat pouring from his bald head.

"If you want this freedom I'm talking about, you don't have to jump through a flaming hula hoop. You don't have to turn no backward flips. All you have to do is accept Christ as your Lord and Savior and you will never have to see another day locked up or locked down again, for that matter. Everybody, stand to your feet. Let's give Him some praise," the preacher says.

The boys stand up and begin to clap their hands. The word was so strong and powerful. The officer's praised God too. Some of the boys were touched, because some of them had tears rolling down their cheeks.

"With every head down, let us pray. Now, if you been saved before and you done back slid, come on up. Or if you need a special prayer step up. If you haven't ever been saved and you want to change your ways, come up. Don't worry about who is looking at you. If you want special prayer, come on up."

Bobby and his brother went up for prayer. This was the first time Bobby had seen his brother since the high speed chase. They both agreed it was a great service and they are happy to see one another.

After church service was over, the residents were escorted back to their rooms. For the next 2 ½ hours the residents cleaned up the whole unit, including their rooms, showers and dayroom. Bobby wasn't too fond of this idea at all. After the unit cleaning was done, all the residents came out their rooms for an hour of recreation and leisure time.

Bobby seemed to be surprised, to see how relaxed everyone seemed to be while they were locked up. It was as though these kids seemed to forget where they were. The scene was like a big community center, everyone running around having a good ole time. Much different from when he first arrived.

The outside recreation area was a big open field, where the boys often ran and played football on one side and on the other side was a basketball court. It was surrounded by 20 feet fences, with sharp barbwire at the top.

The signs clearly and boldly said, "Do not touch and do not attempt to cross." That barbwire was something serious. While on the rec yard, Bobby's thoughts were interrupted.

"Hey shawty. What's up? What's yo name is?" a deep voice called out behind him.

Bobby turned to the direction the voice came from.

"Um Bobby," he answered. "What's yo name?"

"Rudy," the boy replied. "Um from that CP nigga. What you know bout College Park?" he asks, as he smiles with his right index finger in the air.

"I been to CP before. It's cool," said Bobby.

"Where you from?" Rudy asked.

"I'm from LA, but I live in Atlanta now," said Bobby.

Rudy is a rough neck originally from Atlanta inner city. He stands 6' and weighs about 200 lbs. He's definitely a big kid. He has been in and out of juvenile since he was about 13 years old. He really wasn't a bad kid; he just came from a bad environment. He has a good heart and is always respectful towards staff and others.

The two boys hit it off good. The two talked for the remaining of rec time. Bobby seemed to be relieved, to have someone to talk to. Later at rec, he saw his brother Anthony. The brothers were happy to see each other despite the situation. Anthony explained, how apologetic he was about stealing their mom's car: the high speed chase and the wreck. He also expressed his regret about killing the little girl, the one thing he regretted the most. Anthony also told Bobby, how much he hated being locked up. They both talked about how much they both missed home and their mom.

I think it was safe to say, that Anthony seemed to be really sorry for what he had done and the pain he had caused. He realized he was in a lot of trouble. He had made the mistake of his life. He also told his little brother that he told the police, his mother and everybody else, that his brother had nothing to do with what happened. He assured Bobby that he told everyone even the Judge, which was Judge Roberts, that Bobby was totally innocent.

Rec was over and they hugged each other. Anthony reassured Bobby that he would be going home soon and he did not have anything to worry about. Of course, this made Bobby feel so much better about the situation.

Later that night after shower time, during leisure Bobby and Rudy picked up their conversation from earlier at the rec yard. The other boys in the dayroom were watching TV and playing board games. The two boys were in their own world. Bobby told Rudy that he had seen his brother. He was surprised to find out that Bobby had a brother that was locked up with him.

Rudy asked Bobby, "what's your brother's name?"

"Anthony Berry. He's on D unit." Bobby replied.

"He on my unit. I think I seen him earlier," Rudy said.

Rudy proceeded to ask more questions, "why you in here?"

"I'm here for something my stupid brother did. He was charged with vehicular homicide and stealing my mom's car. (UVMV). He was running from the police, he hit and killed a girl. And ain't no telling what else he got charged with," Bobby explained.

"Shawty, your brother did the damn thing... that's fucked up. Whose sister he hit and kill?" asks Rudy, with this crazy look on his face.

"Well... it was a little girl. I think they said, she was about six or seven," Bobby said sadly.

"Damn!" Rudy interrupted.

"All this happened right by my school," Bobby said, as his eyes looked around the dayroom.

Then Rudy asked Bobby, "where you go to school?"

"I go to Douglass Middle," Bobby responded.

"What they charged you with?" Rudy continues to ask with curiosity.

"I was charged with accessory to UVMV and vehicular homicide. I didn't have anything to do with the mess," Bobby said, as if he was getting angry just thinking about it.

"You was in the car with him?" Rudy asked, "shawty you shouldn't have been riding with him."

 "Let me tell you the real, what really happened," Bobby paused and took a deep breath.

 Just as he did, a voice called out, "count time. Let's go. Everybody go to your door, it's now count time."

 "Let's go!" another officer added.

"Rudy- once count is clear, I'm going to let you know what really went down."

 Bobby was excited to share his story with Rudy. Up until now, no one wanted to listen to his side of the story, so it felt good to Bobby that somebody wanted to listen to him and let him get it off his chest.

 All the boys complied with the officer's requests and went to their rooms with no problem. After the 30 minute count was cleared; the boys were allowed to resume their leisure time.   Just as Bobby had promised he and Rudy resumed their conversation.

"So, like I was telling you, this is the truth about what happened," Bobby said looking at Rudy.

 Just then Anthony came over to say what's up to his little brother.

"What up Bobby?" Anthony said, as he sat down and shook his brother's hand.

"What's up Anthony?" Bobby replied with a big smile.

"Shit!" Anthony said, in a low voice, "trying to survive around this muthafucka."

"I know right.   This is Rudy.   My homeboy from College Park.   I was telling him about you," Bobby say's looking at both boys.

 Anthony paused for a moment, as he checked Rudy out.   Then he gave Rudy a fist bump. "What's up pimp?" Anthony says, with a slight smile.

"What happening with it?" Rudy returns the gestor with smile.

"Hey shawty. Yo little brother is cool like a muthafucka."

"That's my nigga," Anthony said, proudly.

"Hey Bobby, I'll hit you up later shawty." Anthony says, as he begins to get up from his chair raising his hand for permission to move. That's the thing in the detention center, there's no movement without permission.

"Alright," Bobby says, as he reaches out to give his brother a little dap. Then Bobby turns back to Rudy excited to tell his part of the story.

"So, um getting ready to walk home from school right."

"Right," Rudy replied, listening to his every word.

"Man, I remember it was so hot outside. It felt like it was 900 degrees outside. So, um about to start walking home. Then, the next thing I know, I see my mom's black Mercedes pulling up, now um thinking, cool- I don't have to walk in this heat. So, when she pulled up, I jumped in the car. Well, I could not see who was driving, because my mom's car window tent is so dark, you can't see inside it. My mama's windows are mobbed out. When I get in the car, it's not my mama driving, it's my brother! As soon as I sit down, this dummy pulls off. I was like man, why you driving mom's car? He come talking bout sum mama let me drive. I knew he was lying, cause he don't even have no driver's license. He started driving all crazy. I promise you Rudy, the whole time he was driving crazy, I begged him to let me out that car. Man, I knew something bad was gone happen and that's the whole truth and nothing but the truth. Real talk. I put that on everything."

Rudy was quiet, his eyes grew big. "Wow! Damn you know what shawty? I believe you."

"Rudy, um not lying to you," Bobby said, as he stared with a blank look.

"Damn shawty, that's fucked up."

"What you think they gone do to me?" he asked with a serious concern look on his face.

"Is this your first offense?" Rudy asked.

"Yes. I've never been in any kind of trouble in my life. I make straight A's in school," Bobby said, sounding convincing.

"If yo brother tells the judge, that he took yo mom's car and you just had got out of school and he picked you up, you should be straight."

"Yeah, my brother said that he already told the police, my mama and the judge about what happened."

"You going home shawty. You straight!" said Rudy.

Bobby felt relieved to hear Rudy say, he should be going home soon. Then Rudy asked him, "when yo court date is?"

"I go to court on Monday, that's tomorrow," Bobby said with a smile.

Bobby felt good about his day in court.

"White cards!" Officer Johnson yells.

"It is eight o'clock. All white cards go to your doors. It's bed time."

"Officer Hill, I didn't get my nu-nu yet," Eddy says, like a little 5 year old.

"If you don't move...with yo breathe smelling like money ass," Officer Hill says.

The whole dayroom just busted out laughing. Eddy is a big tough boy by day, but acts like a complete child, by night. He acts like a 3-year-old and trust me Eddy has a way of working the officer's nerves.

"I don't like him," Eddy says, as he points at Officer Hill.

"He's mean," he adds.

"Um mean to dumb muthafuckas," Officer Hill responses.

"Um gone bring the snacks to y'all door." Officer Parker says, to the boys trying not to laugh in his face.

Bobby told Rudy and Anthony good night and headed to his room.

That night, Bobby prayed and prayed for the good Lord to let him go home. Bobby was so excited about going to court and possibly going home, he could not sleep at all, or it might have been all the banging and yelling on the unit.

Residents were talking under the doors and rapping loud all night long. Again, Bobby stayed awake, half the night tossing and turning. Thoughts of his court date danced in his head. He also thought about, what he was going to do, when he got out of juvenile hall. He went to sleep believing, in his heart of heart, he was going home to his mother tomorrow.

CHAPTER 5

THE COURT DATE

"Wake up, wake up!" the officer's yells, as they bang on the doors to awake the residents. The officer's loud voices alarmed Bobby and the others. He wakes up startled and feeling like he had been partying all night, but he was excited, because today is a big day for him. It's Monday morning and its Bobby's big court day. He was going home; he could just feel it in his skinny bones.

Bobby is shuffled to breakfast with about 25 others residents. He looks for his brother in the dining area, but does not see him. He thought to himself, Anthony must have skipped breakfast. He sat at the table to eat his breakfast.

"What up shawty?" a voice calls out from behind Bobby. It was Rudy, coming into the dining area. Just then, an officer followed behind Rudy and called off a number of names, from his court list. Bobby was one of the names he called. He grabbed his unfinished breakfast tray and got in line with the other residents.

"Good luck," Rudy says, as Bobby is leaving the dining area for court.

"Everything gone be alright shawty," Rudy adds with a smile.

"Alright then," Bobby replies, as he smiles back at Rudy.

The residents are escorted to the intake area. They are shackled down and loaded on the transportation bus.

That morning, Bobby went to court before the judge. The judge's name was Judge Roberts. He was an old white man with snow white hair. He looked like he had been around since the early 1800s and he was known for being rude and straight to the point. He didn't cut no corners.

Bobby stood in front of Judge Roberts shaking like a leaf on a tree in a winter storm, that's what he does when he is scared. Sweat beads started to drip off his forehead. He sees his mother, but that did little to calm his nerves. Judge Roberts stared down at Bobby through his glasses. The way judge Roberts looked down at him from the high bench, made him feel even more nervous and very intimidated.

Judge Roberts asked Bobby a number of questions. He was so nervous; he could barely talk. He struggled and stumbled all over his words. His voice cracked like booming thunder. He never had to stand in front of a judge before. This was his first and hopefully his last time. Bobby's voice weakened as he spoke to the judge in low tone.

"Speak up son!" Judge Roberts roared.

Bobby clammed up and tried not to make eye contact with the judge. It seemed like his eyes were in roam mode. Bobby felt like he might as well be going to the electric chair, because it sure seemed like it.

When it was all said and done, needless to say, things didn't go as good as Bobby had planned. In fact, it was a flat out disappointment for him. The judge had already heard the testimony from Anthony and the judge already knew about Bobby and his good grades and all. But the bottom line was, he was in a stolen car that hit and killed an innocent little girl, so somebody had to pay.

Bobby had it in his mind that on this day, he was going home and when he learned that he wasn't, he was upset. Bobby cried uncontrollable right on the

spot. Tears rolled down his face. Snot ran from his
nose. He used his shirt to wipe his face and tried to
keep his big boy on. But, the tears kept falling and his
nose kept running. He was so hurt. He didn't want to
go back to that nasty filthy detention center.

The judge took it in consideration, that this was
Bobby's first time in trouble. He also considered what
Anthony had told him; that Bobby didn't have any
involvement in the incident that happened. He felt he
was a good kid, so the judge considered giving him a
second chance. Bobby really felt that he was being
held and punished for no reason at all. So, needless to
say he wasn't happy about the judge findings.

Bobby knew in his mind he had done nothing wrong,
but what else was he going to do. What else could he
do? Nothing, but accept it and take it like a man and
that's exactly what he did. He took his sentence like a
brave young man and decided to make the best out of
the situation.

He watched the other boys go home, while he had to
return back to the juvenile detention center. Seeing
the other kids go home, only made things tough.
When Bobby returned back to the facility, the
residents was already at rec. Although Bobby

received 60 days in detention, he realized that things could have been a whole lot worse. He wasn't much in the mood for rec, but he went any away.

"Hey shawty. You going home? What's happening?" Rudy asked, with ridiculous excited look on his face, as Bobby entered the rec yard.

"Nall, um still here," said Bobby, with his head down.

Rudy's smile quickly disappeared. "What the judge tell you, what's up?"

"Judge Roberts gave me 60 day's in here," Bobby says, as he tucked his hands underneath his grey t-shirt and flopped himself on the grass crossing his legs. He leaned back on the fence to support his back.

"60 days!" Rudy says, aloud, "nigga... 60 days... shit that's gravy than uh- mutha fucka."

Then Rudy went on to say, "I wish I had only 60 days. I'll do that shit standing on my head, foe real shawty. You know how much time I got in this bitch?"

"How much?"

"I got 120 months from the floor to the door, that's 10 year's my nigga. Man you ought to be happy, you going home in two months," Rudy says, trying to perk his friend up.

"I know, but I didn't even do nothing... I'm innocent. I thought for sho I was going home today."

Then Rudy says to Bobby, "well since you gone be here for a minute, I got yo back. If one of these lame ass niggas try you, just let me know. I'll beat one of these niggas ass, real talk shawty. These niggas ain't ready shawty."

Bobby looked at Rudy and said, "I appreciate that, but I think I'm gone be cool," Bobby replied with a smile.

"You know the reason why I got 120 months?" Rudy asked.

"It's because you really did it huh," Bobby said.

"Hell yeah nigga, I'm guilty like a muthafucka," said Rudy.

The boys both laughed. Just then Anthony approached them.

"What happened at court today?" Anthony asked Bobby.

"What's up Rudy?"

"What up Ant?"

"Well, the judge gave me two months," Bobby says.

"60 more days! Man I'm sorry I got you in the fuck shit, but I thought they were gone let you go to the crib. That's fucked up shawty," said his older brother feeling sorry for the time and trouble he got his younger innocent brother in.

"I ain't tripping. I'm just gone do what they tell me to do, keep myself busy and keep my mind right," said Bobby. "It's all good," he added.

Just then the sound of a whistle filled the air, followed by the officer demanding the residents to line up, because the hour of rec is over.

Later that evening during dinner, a couple of boys attempted to take Bobby's food. It's was Tony and his crew. Tony is a bad boy. He's been in and out of juvenile since he was twelve years old. He is now 17 going on 35, and he thinks he knows it all. He has a few flunkies that does any and everything that he tells them to. His so called boys are Marcus 16, Larry 16 and Patrick 15, and none of them are smart enough to think for themselves. The only thing they want to do is impress Tony.   All he does is disrespect them and boss them around all day.

   Tony is originally from Chicago, but has been living in Forest Park with his grandmother, (a small city just outside of Atlanta) since he was 8 years old. Tony isn't anything, but a big bully. All day long, he and his funky crew walk around trying to find someone to bother. Tony is a big kid. He is about 6'2 and 285 pounds. So, he uses his size to intimidate others.

   As Rudy comes in from medical with Officer Hill, he noticed Tony and his crew giving Bobby a hard time and trying to take his tray.

   "Man why y'all niggas trying my lil potna. Y'all lame ass niggas beta get right," Rudy says in a loud and angry tone with his fist balled up, as if he was ready to throw down at any minute.

   Just then, the officer intervened to break the boys up. Tony and his boys were surprised that Rudy had stood up for Bobby. And truth be told, Bobby was just as surprised as well. Tony didn't say a word, as they backed up. Rudy shut them all down.

"Give my nigga his shit back!" Rudy ordered, as he reaches over to Tony taking Bobby's tray back from him. "Bitch ass nigga," Rudy added looking at Tony dead in his eyes; as if he was saying to himself, do something nigga. I wish you would try some shit.

The officers tell Rudy to stop cussing and chill out, redirecting his negative behavior.

"Matter fact, since ya'll want to be starting shit, I should take y'all shit," Rudy said.

Tony was embarrassed. Rudy completely shut him down in front of his boys and in front of everybody else. The officers acted like they really didn't want to get involved.

"Rudy sit down, leave them alone before I put you in your room," said officer Hill.

The other officers told the boys to stop acting up.

"Tell them lames not to be trying my lil partna like that," Rudy said.

Bobby sat there at the table looking in total shock. To all the boys in the dining area, the message was very clear. Don't mess with Bobby Berry or you gone have to deal with Rudy.

CHAPTER 6

BACK IN GENERAL POPULATION

Several days had passed, since the dining room incident when Tony and his crew tried to take Bobby's food tray. Once Tony seen that Rudy had Bobby's back, they didn't want no parts of that. You see, Tony was tough, but Rudy was just as tough.

Rudy had a reputation for knocking dudes out and everybody knew that he didn't take no junk, from no body. The difference between Tony and Rudy was that, Rudy wasn't a bully and didn't need no lame crew like Tony did. Tony was nothing, but a bully and he wouldn't bust a grape without his crew.

In the meanwhile, it has been several days since the last time Bobby has seen his brother Anthony until this day.

"Hey Anthony, where you been?" asked Bobby, as he flopped down next to him at leisure time.

"What's up Bobby? I been on lock down shawty."

"Lock down, for what?" Bobby asked, surprisingly.

"Shawty… it's a long story," Anthony says, as he put his right hand on his head and he takes a deep breath. He goes on to explain to Bobby what happened, then he looked around and across the dayroom, as to make sure the conversation he and his brother was having was private. Anthony drew closer to Bobby.

"You know that little girl I hit by accident when I was on the high speed chase?"

 Bobby nods his head and says, "Yeah," as he listened to Anthony with interest and he wanted him to explain more.

 "Well… the boy I got into a fight with, is the girl's cousin."

 Bobby's jaw dropped, he leaned back with his hand over his mouth, and his eyes were as big as a silver dollar.

"Dang!" Bobby said, with much surprise.

"Are you serious?" Bobby asked.

 "Hell yeah, that's fucked up ain't it?"

 "Yeah!" Bobby replied, still looking surprised.

"Are you sure? What's the girl's cousin name?"

"That lame ass nigga name is Tony."

"Tony!" Bobby said, burying his face in his hands.

"He's the one that was trying to bully me the other day."

"Nigga what... shawty!" Anthony said, as he balled up his fist. "Nigga, I'm ma beat that nigga ass. Bitch ass mutherfucka. I put that on everything shawty."

Bobby proceeded to tell Anthony how Rudy looked after him.

"How did Tony find out about what happened?" Bobby asked. Then all of a sudden, like a rush of wind, Officer Johnson's name came to Bobby's mind.

"I don't know shawty, but I don't trust that nigga Officer Johnson for shit. He probably the one that told him," Anthony says in an elevating tone.

"I haven't told nobody about it, have you?" Anthony asked Bobby.

"No, I wouldn't be telling that. I have no idea how he knows, but somehow he found out. Well, I did tell

Rudy what happened, but I know he wouldn't tell anyone else."

Bobby paused for a moment, and then said, "I didn't tell nobody else besides Rudy." He answered, as he stared off into space, as if he was trying to remember if he had told somebody about it or not. "Naw, that's it. He the only one I told."

Then Anthony gave Bobby a serious look and said, "don't tell nobody in here that you my little brother, because if they find out we brothers, they gone fuck with you. You feel me? Don't tell these niggas shit shawty, you feel me?" Anthony says, as he looks straight into his only brother's eyes.

"I told Rudy that we was brothers, but he's the only one and I already know he not gone tell nobody. I feel you bruh. I promise not to tell anybody else," Bobby replied.

"Just know I ain't gone let these niggas fuck with you, that's real."

There's a group of boys playing cards sitting at the table just behind them. The noise gets their attention, they both pause for a minute to see what the noise was about.

"Y'all at the back table! Y'all too damn loud!" Officer Simms yelled from across the room.

"My bad Officer Simms. We'll be quiet."

The boys bring the noise to a minimum.

"Sorry I got you caught up in this shit, lil bruh," Anthony said.

 Bobby was happy to see and talk to his brother again. Bobby and Anthony talked about a lot of things, but mostly about Bobby staying safe. Anthony told Bobby he was facing 15 to 20 years for his wrong doing, but despite that Anthony felt really bad about killing that little girl and getting his little brother in so much trouble. He also told Bobby not to get into any trouble and to keep his mind on getting out of jail and making something of his life.

 Bobby promised Anthony that he would not fight or get in trouble and that he would make something out of his life.

CHAPTER 7

RUDY

The next few days seemed like eternity. The days went by slow and the nights even slower. Day in and day out, all Bobby could think about was going home and being with his mother.

One day during rec time, Bobby was sitting alone by himself reading a book, when Tony and his crew approached him. They decided they wanted to pick on him. Rudy nor Anthony was nowhere to be seen. Tony grabbed his book, and then began to play a game of keep away with his boys.

"Give me my book back!" Bobby demanded, in a stern voice.

Tony and his crew ignored his request and kept throwing his book around. The next thing you know, Rudy appeared out of nowhere. He calmly walked over to Tony and his crew.

"Y'all muthafuckas don't read. Give him his book back!" Rudy demanded.

Tony and his crew all looked at each other, not to mention they looked surprised by Rudy's presence. Give the fucking book back to shawty," Rudy demanded angry, as he stepped closer to Tony and his boys. They all paused and looked at each other with a puzzled look on their faces.

"What you gone do if we don't?" Tony asked Rudy.

By this time, the residents on the rec yard started walking over to see what the commotion was about.

"Uma whoop you and them lame ass niggas ass." The next thing you know Rudy begin to square off with Tony and the other boys.

"Rudy! It's ok. Don't worry about it. It's not worth it," Bobby calls out trying to stop Rudy from fighting.

Now, there is a small crowd around gassing the boys up to fight. Cheers quickly filled the air. "Bet you want fire on that nigga ass." Followed with more fighting words.

"If you want the book nigga, get it with- yo- mutha-fucking- muscles," said Tony, with his boys behind him.

The others boys begin to circle around Rudy with their fists balled up ready to fight. Bobby backs up trying to keep his promise to his brother; not to fight. The next thing you know, Tony suddenly ran up on Rudy without notice throwing a vicious right. Rudy ducks the right hand blow. Then he came up with a left hand blow that connected with Tony's jaw. It rocked him like a hurricane. Tony's body instantly went limp, dropping him to the ground. It was a TKO. He was laid out, face down.

"Damn!" the crowd echoed, followed by, "oooh!"

"Lights out, like ah mutha-fucka!" another boy yelled aloud, waving his arms and standing over Tony making a knocked out gestor, like a boxing referee.

Tony was knocked out with his eyes closed, he wasn't moving. "Night, night for you, face ass nigga," another boy called from the crowd.

Rudy had caught Tony with a one hitter quitter. Tony was done. Everyone gasped when Rudy connected to Tony's jaw. You could hear the lick a mile away.

The other two boys rushed Rudy at the same time. By now, everyone on the rec yard was spectating and edging them on.

"Fight! Fight! Fight!" the crowd chanted in perfect unison.

The crowd yelled, "beat that nigga ass!"

While others yelled, "kick his ass!"

The whole crowd was cheering them on.

What these young boys didn't know was that Rudy was a black belt in Martial Arts. They had no idea who they was messing with. Larry and Marcus rushed Rudy. All you seen was Rudy kicking, spinning, and throwing vicious blows, and he wasn't missing.

It was two against one and they could not handle Rudy. He beat both them boys up. Rudy busted Marcus lip and give Larry a black eye. "Damn, that nigga eye is on twenty- two's," one boy commented. When Patrick seen how Rudy worked them hands, he didn't want none. He took off running. Turns out Patrick wasn't so dumb after all. After about two or three minutes of good old fashion butt whipping, the officers on the rec yard called a 10-10 code (which means fight).

Officer Johnson was the first officer to arrive on the scene of the fight, followed by Officer Simms and Officer Coleman. I'm sure that Larry and Marcus was happy to see the officers coming, because Rudy was beating the brakes off both of them, like they stole something.

Once the officers arrived, they grabbed the boys and pulled them apart, thus breaking up the big fight. Everyone that wasn't involved in the fight was ordered to lay face down, while the officers sort things out.

While the situation was being taking care of, all the boys on the rec yard complied with the officer's directives.

"Yeah nigga... this shit ain't over," Tony says to Rudy, as he was waking up from being knocked the hell out. While he was talking trash, he was protected by the other officer's presence.

"Nigga you PC stunin," says Rudy. "Stop flexin shawty," he added, while looking down at Tony.

"Hey! It's over!" one officer yells.

"Y'all leave that shit alone," Another officer adds, as they escort all four boys off the rec yard. Once the four fighters are in their rooms, Officer Johnson starts to write the report, because he was the first to arrive on the scene. The officers go back outside, to bring in the remaining group.

"Rec is over!" the officers announced.

"Line up! We going in!" another officer joined in.

The kids muttered, as they reluctantly complied. Now, Officer Johnson is a very shady character. He was the kind of person you could not trust. He was a dark skin fellow, with a short haircut. He stood about 6'1 or 6'2. This guy was definitely a piece of work. He worked at Fuller JDC for about three years, before he came over to Freeman JDC. He has worked there as an officer for about four years now.

For some reason, most seem to believe that Officer Johnson and the Director, Mr. Boykin are family, because they are so tight. After the big show down, all four boys were written up and were placed on confinement.

Two days later, guess who showed up for breakfast? Everyone that was involved in the fight, except Rudy. When Bobby saw this, not only did he fear for his safety, but he knew this wasn't right. The fact that Anthony was at breakfast made Bobby feel a little better.

I mean Bobby was there from start to finish and seen the whole thing go down, but Officer Johnson didn't ask him no questions or even what happened. Heck, Officer Johnson didn't even ask any of the boys out there to write a witness statement about the fight. This just seems to be fishy to Bobby. The main one who caused the fight was out, but Rudy is facing three additional charges.

This did not go over well with Bobby, especially the fact that Rudy was just trying to help him out. Bobby felt like he had to do something. What? He didn't know. He just knew he had to do something. Bobby felt that Officer Johnson had something to do with this.

Now that Rudy was on lock down, Tony and his crew knew that they could pick on Bobby every chance they got. And they did just that, just not in front of Anthony. After Tony fought Anthony, he had respect for him. He found out that Anthony wasn't just a push over, but trust me Tony had some plans for him. Big plans. But in the meantime, Tony and his crew harassed Bobby. They took his food and snacks away, when his brother wasn't around. Some days Bobby didn't even eat. Tony even told Bobby that if he told anyone, he promised he would beat him down.

Bobby felt belittled, violated and scared. He didn't know what to do or who to tell. He wanted to tell Anthony, but he didn't want him trying to fight and end up in more trouble on his account. Bobby just took Tony's crap. Whenever Anthony would ask Bobby how things were going, he would always tell him, everything was all good. He didn't tell his brother what was really going on. Bobby just kept counting the days he had left and kept his mind occupied with thoughts of going home. He held on to his brother's words of wisdom "Don't fight... Go home."

CHAPTER 8

COUNSELING SESSION

The boys waited patiently in the dayroom for Mr. Manning's counseling session to begin. Mr. Manning is the counselor at Freeman JDC. He's a strong, stern man and he's the type of guy that gets straight to the point.

Mr. Manning was in his mid-30s, a college graduate with a master degree. He stands about 5'8" and his belly suggests he drinks a lot of beer. Just about every day, Mr. Manning shows up to work smelling like he just left the neighborhood bar and today was no exception.

He walks into the unit. The dayroom is full with residents anticipating what he will be talking about today. As he walks through the door, the boys quietly turn around. He makes his way to the front of the dayroom, next to the TV.

"First of all, shut the hell up," said Mr. Manning to the quiet group.

The group of looked confused, because no was talking. One hand goes up, Mr. Manning looks.

"And what do you want?" asked Mr. Manning.

"You told us to shut up. Ain't nobody even talking."

"I said that before y'all start talking. Just be quiet and here what I got to say," he said, as he stared back at the boys with blood shot red eyes.

"What's your name?" Mr. Manning asked a resident sitting on the front row.

"Bobby," he said.

"Bobby, what's yo last name?"

"Berry."

Then Mr. Manning eyes focused back on the group.

"Alright, for everybody that don't know who I am. I am Mr. Manning. I'm your counselor. The first thing I want y'all to do is take a good look around," he says, as he looks over the group. "Go ahead. Look around tell me what you see?" he asks, then he paused waiting for a response.

"A bunch of lames," one resident says.

"Anyway, I see a room full of young black men," another resident says.

"Exactly!" Expels Mr. Manning, "not a bunch of niggas like y'all like to call y'all selves. But a room full of smart and intelligent young men; that make stupid decisions. It's a shame out of the majority of you all, most of y'all are black."

Mr. Manning went on explain how much money the state is making off the residents.

"Y'all running around in here like y'all cool. Y'all asses ain't cool. Y'all some fools, excuse my French. I know I'm not supposed to be cussing and using that kind of language, but some of you all curse worse than I do. Somebody need to tell y'all stupid asses the truth. I'm gone to tell you whose cool, that dude y'all be calling lame. That's who's cool." The residents observing him looking around at each other.

"Y'all know why that lame dude is cool, cause he ain't getting locked up like y'all ass. He ain't walking around trying to act hard, like y'all dumb ass. That lame dude is somewhere free and y'all ass are in here, locked up and can't even stay out of jail. Y'all wearing somebody nasty ass draws, but y'all cool. I know some of y'all shouldn't be here, but that same dude y'all calling a nerd and a lame somewhere free, reading a book, learning something and handling his business. Hell- most of y'all can't even read a damn book." Mr. Manning says, to the group of boys. Some boys gasped and others looked angry at the man.

"True message though, I don't care about you getting mad, but y'all cool," the counselor added.

"He straight on that Malcom X shit," Tony whispered with his head down.

"Close your mouth!" Officer Coleman advises, "you the main one that needs to be listening," he added.

"If you don't want to listen, carry your ass to yo room," says Mr. Manning.

"I'm gone tell you the truth. I don't care if you get mad. You all are wasting the best time of y'all life away. There's so many other things that you all could be doing besides getting locked up. All y'all got talent. Some of y'all are good in sports. I've seen him run," Mr. Manning says, as he points to one of the boys sitting up front, "this mutha-fucka fast. I know you turned yourself in, cause the police wasn't gone to catch yo ass."

The group of boys laugh. Then Mr. Manning says, "sports might not be your thing, but everybody in here got something they can do. 85% of all y'all been here more than three or four times and that's a damn shame."

Then Mr. Manning pauses. "Why y'all keep coming back to jail? Y'all act like this the shit!"

"Hell nah," a few boys mumbled.

"Listen... when y'all go home, try some different shit. Stop robbing people, stop stealing and shooting folks. Do something different. Hell, try something positive. A famous poet said, "You will never arrive at a different destination, if you always take the same path."

"Some of y'all may not understand that, but what he was saying is, if you do the same thing you gone get the same results. Most of y'all get out of jail and go back doing the same stupid shit. I don't understand that."

Bobby raised his hand.

"You have a question or a comment?" Mr. Manning asked.

"Yes sir. I read about positive information when I'm at home," says, Bobby.

"You all need to read more," Mr. Manning says looking at the group of boys. "When you read you get informed. Information rules the nation. Information is key. Information is knowledge and knowledge is power. I know y'all tired of hearing me talking. I'm bout done, but I need to tell you boys how y'all getting played by the system. Little do you all know, but the systems don't want y'all to go home and get right. Why? Because y'all they bread and butter. Like I said before, these folks getting paid off y'all. It's pathetic! So, when they give y'all these 30 to 60 days on probation, y'all think that's gravy. They already know you going to be back to the same old hood, to the same friends, same environment; which is going to result in the same situation. In other words, nine times out of ten, yo ass will be right back and they already know this. Violate that probation and see what's gone happen. They got two-ten years waiting fo yo ass. If not mo. If you jay walk while you on yo probation, they gone lock yo ass back up. They gone give you one to five years for jay walking. That probation shit ain't gravy, not at all. It's a trap and that's all it is. You all get good and religious when you in jail, but when the good Lord blesses you to get out, you don't even say thank you. You forget all about how God blessed you to get out. But one thing about God, he's still here when you get back. One other thing, you may forget about God, but God won't forget about you. When you leave here, take God with you. Get in church when you go home. Stop being a thug and hanging with thugs. If you running with thugs, you gone be a thug. The bible says, "...birds of a feather flock together."

"Get some positive friends. Hell... get some lame friends. If you don't change your ways, you gone end up dead or be somebody's bitch in the pen. Excuse my French, but that's real. I didn't come here to be bullshiting with y'all... um here to tell you the truth, whether you like it or not. I love you dumb muthafuckas. I know I talk a lot of shit, but I do love y'all for real. I shole don't do this for the money. I do this because of y'all!"

Then Mr. Manning paused, taking a deep breath. "Alright officers, I appreciate y'all time. You boys be good," he says, as he gathers his things off the table to exit the day room unit.

The officers on the unit, instructed the boys to go to their doors to get prepared for shower time.

"Alright listen up!" Officer Johnson says, as he stands in front of the day room.

"Tonight during shower time, I will be doing phone calls on C unit, so if you want a phone call, you better act like it and keep this damn room quiet."

"Yes sirrrr!" One resident shout out like an army soldier.

Bobby was very excited to get a phone call, because he had not spoken to his mother for some time now and missed her very much. So, needless to say, he couldn't wait and he was looking forward to that phone call. In the Berry House, phone calls were made twice a week and the phone calls were conducted by halls. For an example; C hall had phone calls every Tuesday and the other halls would rotate later in the week.

These were free phone calls. The officer's regulated the phone calls. The staff would get the phone out of the office, located near the gym and would allow the residents to make a five minute phone call. Again, this was C hall time to make calls.

Midway through showers, Officer Johnson started the phone calls for C-hall. Bobby was in C hall room 06.

Officer Johnson sat outside of the shower and watched, while the residents made their phone calls. The other officers watched the residents, while they quietly played games and watched TV, in the dayroom. Officer Johnson was able to do showers and watch the residents at the same time.

Bobby waited patiently for his turn to use the phone. He was so anxious he could not set still. After about 20 minutes, Officer Johnson calls for the next person to use the phone. He also announces that this would be the last phone call for the night.

Bobby stood up and made his way to the phone, as he did, Tony jumped up too.

"Tony!" Officer Johnson, called from the shower area.

Bobby was still walking towards Officer Johnson.

"Sit down!" he said, as he handed the phone to Tony.

"But I'm on C hall. I'm supposed to have a phone call tonight."

"Boy, if you don't sit your narrow ass down..." Officer Johnson said, to Bobby.

"Bet that up," Tony says, as he grabs the phone, giving Bobby an evil smile.

"How he getting a phone call, when he had a call just yesterday? He ain't even on C hall. He on D hall," Bobby says, pleading his case with tears running down his face.

"Boy, if you don't sit your narrow ass down. I'm gone slap yo ass back to yesterday," he says, raising his voice and giving Bobby a shove. "Go to your room!" the cunning officer demanded.

"I haven't spoken to my mother on the phone, only one time since I been here. Please just let me say, hello to her," Bobby pleaded with tears pouring from his eyes.

"Boy go to your damn room!" says Officer Johnson, pointing again in the direction of his room.

"That's not right!" Bobby responded, as he marched down the hall to his room.

Then Officer Johnson suddenly rushed over to Bobby, grabbed him by the arm and roughly escorted him to his room and locked the door. Everything in the dayroom stopped and it got quiet. All of the sudden,

Officer Johnson walked back to the dayroom, cut off the TV and said out loud, "I run this muthafucka and don't y'all forget that shit!"

Bobby was angry and embarrassed about what happened in front of everybody. He cried his self to sleep that night. He knew he didn't do anything to deserve that kind of treatment and disrespect from Officer Johnson. He was really angry and hurt at the same time.

The next day, Bobby wasn't sure about what to do regarding the phone incident or even who to tell for that matter. He remembered reading the student handbook which said, if any residents have problems with any other residents or staff, write a grievance letter, and the matter will be looked into. So, that's exactly what Bobby did. He wrote a grievance on Officer Johnson and he spelled out the whole incident word for word. He even wrote about how Officer Johnson cursed him out, grabbed him by the arm and locked him in his room for no reason.

In the grievance, he also wrote how Officer Johnson gave Tony a ten-minute phone call when everybody else received only five minutes. This was showing favoritism. Bobby wrote all about how he was denied his right to make a phone call for no apparent reason. Not only did he write a grievance, he also went to the counselor, Mr. Manning and told him about the whole situation.

Mr. Manning felt sorry for Bobby so, he allowed him to make a phone call from his office. Mr. Manning could not believe what he had told him. Bobby called his mother and told her how Officer Johnson cursed him out, denied his phone call and put his hands on him. His mother hit the roof when he told her how he was treated. She instantly become irate.

The next day, Bobby's mother was there in the Mr. Boykin's office raising hell. She also made several phone calls down to the juvenile justice department, which was located down town Atlanta. Some heads was going to roll. Bobby's mother put pressure on Mr. Boykin to have Officer Johnson dealt with and she wasn't backing down until someone took action about him and his behavior.

The following day Mr. Boykin called Officer Johnson to his office and shredded him to pieces with his words. After he chewed him up and spit him out. Officer Johnson was written up and suspended for five days. (They call that, getting put in the streets) Mr.

Boykin told Officer Johnson, the next time he heard him doing anything to the kids; of any kind of wrong he would be fired on the spot. Period. Point blank.

 As you know that did not go over well with Officer Johnson. All these years he had been with J.D.C. He had never been written up. Now, he has a suspension. His plans for becoming a supervisor was now shot to hell and he didn't like that. Officer Johnson had a trick up his sleeve. He felt like he had to get Bobby back and he knew just the person.

 Whispers went on throughout the facility about, how Bobby got Officer Johnson in so much trouble and made him look like a complete fool. After the great fall of Officer Johnson and his embarrassing write up and suspension, he lost a lot of favor with the director. He knew that Bobby wasn't a bad kid. He also knew he wasn't the fighting type, but for some reason he just didn't like Bobby.

 Officer Johnson's plan was to persuade Mr. Boykin to have Rudy and Anthony shipped off as soon as possible, so he could finally get Bobby back for embarrassing him and breaking his window of opportunity to become a sergeant.

In the meantime, once he returned back to work, Officer Johnson had just the person in mind to take care of Bobby; once his protection was out of the way.

CHAPTER 9

RUDY'S GONE!

Bang, bang is the sound that echoes throughout the hall. It's a knock on Bobby's door first thing in the morning. He wakes up slowly. He gets up out of his bed to see who's knocking on his door. As Bobby looks out his window with sleep in his eyes, he sees his boy Rudy.

"What's up bruh?" Rudy asks? with a big smile on his face.

"What's up Rudy? What you doing?" Bobby asked, in a sleepy voice.

"I'm gone shawty!"

"Gone! Gone where? What are you talking about?"

"Man, um going to my placement. Um ready to knock out these little ten years," Rudy said.

"I thought you wasn't leaving for another two months."

"I know shawty. Somehow they got me fast track," Rudy added.

"Alright man, you take care of yourself and thank you for looking out for me," said Bobby with a sleepy smile.

"Alright, Rudy!" the officer called from behind, "it's time to go!" he added.

"Alright bruh, you hold it down. Love you lil bruh," says Rudy, as he walks away from Bobby's door.

Bobby watched as his friend Rudy is escorted off the unit until he disappeared into thin air. Just like that, Rudy was gone. There was never a time when he had a friend like him before. I mean, someone that had his back and never expected something in return.

Bobby felt totally hopeless to see Rudy leaving, but he also felt relieved that he was getting his time started. He knew Rudy was just one step closer to going home to his family.

The following day Bobby went to breakfast. He talked to his brother and told him that Rudy had got transported to his placement. Anthony told his brother to watch his back. Anthony felt that since Tony found out about that accident with his cousin, Tony wanted and was planning revenge. Anthony went on to say that he been hearing whispers and people talking on the down low that Tony and his boys was planning to ride on him. And of course, Anthony already knew that it was only a matter of time that Tony would in fact be coming for him.

The only thing that Bobby could focus on was surviving long enough just to go home. From the looks on his brother's face, he could tell this was serious a situation. He knew that Tony and his crew was no good and this concerned him as well. He not only feared for his life, he also feared for his brother's life. Oh yeah, the boys were right, Officer Johnson did inform Tony about the car accident.

CHAPTER 10

THE SESSION

Once a week or so, Officer Coleman would have these sit down talks with the residents. Most of these talks were very deep. They talked about any and everything. There was laughter at times and at other times there were tears and on some occasions there were both.

Officer Coleman was a good officer and a good man. He was one of those officers that showed the kids that he really cared about them. He had a wife and four kids of his own. Although he was a kind man, he didn't play any games and he didn't take no stuff. He was always firm, fair and consistent.

The residents had nothing but respect for him as a man and an officer. All the kids really looked up to him. He always took time to listen to the boys and tried to encourage them and give them good sound advice. What made him feel good is the fact that the boys seem to listen and appreciate him.

In the moment during the talks, it seemed like they wanted to change. Often times the boys would tell him, if I had a father like you, I wouldn't be locked up. For him to hear a young man tell him this, it was a gift all in its self.

"I just want to know if you don't mind me asking, what are some of the things some of you all did to get in here?" Officer Coleman asked the group.

He looks over the residents with watchful eyes. The dayroom full of boys, it gets quiet. The room is empty of sound. The boys look at each other waiting for someone to respond.

"All that talking y'all be doing, when we want y'all to be quiet, y'all be loud. Now, I asked a question and y'all want to act shy."

Officer Coleman always has a big grin on his face. One boy started to speak out, he struggles to articulate his words.

"Um in the 11th grade... and I was making good grades and everything," he paused as he leaned forward to straighten up his posture, "I had all kinds of colleges looking at me to play football."

"Whatever," one of the boys sitting in the group, said.

"One night, me and my boy went to rob this dope boy in the hood, but when we tried to rob him, he pulled out a gun and shot my boy and killed him. And because I was with him, they charged me with the murder. Now, I have to ten do years."

Then Officer Coleman extended his hand out to the boy and told him, "Sorry about that. You're lost, was my lost too. See that same boy you talking about was here two weeks before that happened. He was my friend too. He got out of jail and got killed. You could have gotten killed too, but God had mercy on you. He speared your life. What's your name?"

"Mike," he replied. He sat back down trying to hold back the tears.

I told you things get deep around here.

Suddenly, the room fell quiet when another a boy began to speak, "um in here because I violated my probation."

"If you don't mind me asking, what did you do and what's your name?" asked Officer Coleman.

"No, I don't mind sharing and my name is William. I was skipping school and I got caught stealing from Walmart."

"Why was you at Walmart stealing?" asked one officer.

"My mama was working all the time and she was never at home. I didn't like school," he said, with a corky smile on his face. "Um gone start going to school like I'm supposed to. I only have 3 more months in here. Um going to get out and start making some better choices. Um not trying to stay behind bars all my life shawty."

"As I listen to you all, you all have some good heads on your shoulders. But y'all got to make some better choices. Think about it, you ditching school that's not gone get you anywhere and when you do come in here, yo butt gone go to school anyway. So, you might as well go to school on the outside. Most of you boys are not thinking. The only thing that most of you are concerned about is impressing your friends. When it boils down to it, you know what? Yo friends gone snitch yo ass out. You already know and if you don't know, you gone find out fast. When it comes down to his ass or yo ass; hell, you might as well cancel Christmas cause yo ass is gone."

"Y'all think this shit is funny, but he's telling y'all the truth. Y'all think yo boy won't snitch. Let them folk's getta talking about some real time, yo boy gone tell every fucking thing he knows," Officer Hill said, in a loud clear voice from the back of the dayroom.

"You dog gone right! Every time! Why you want to look cool in front of your boys when they are locked up just like you? Man for what?" Officer Coleman standing up in front of the day room looking at everyone with a serious look on his face. He's not smiling now. "Man y'all don't know and understand how you all are messing up y'all life. Prison is real. Man they up there rapping and ripping boys apart. Who you gone run and tell?"

He paused for a moment, staring at the group in total silence. The boys listen and observed Officer Coleman with intensity, some even stared as if they were shocked to hear this news.

"Man you got dudes that ain't touched a woman in 20 to 30 years. Shit, some even longer than that and a lot of these prisoners ain't never going home. Most these men in prison will never be close to a woman again. What you think they gone do to you? They won't think twice about taking your man hood and bitching you out." Officer Hill said.

Then Officer Simms abruptly intervene saying, "excuse me Coleman. I just want to say something. Since we talking, y'all know me, I'm gone keep the shit real. What Hill is saying, men in prison they do rape young boys and they don't think twice about it. I hear stories all the time about these boys getting in here and going to prison and getting raped. They don't care, they'll ride yo ass like a Shetland pony."

The boys' eyes grew, then they all turned back around to face Officer Coleman. "Man y'all better wake up and stop taking your life and freedom for a joke. The sad part is, for a lot of y'all half of y'all already facing big boy time. Y'all need to be trying to talk to some of these other boys that already got time. They wish they was in y'all shoes."

Officer Simms interrupts again from behind the group of residents, they turn around to see him as he talks to Officer Coleman. "Officer Coleman you know what um gone do?"

"What's that?" asked Officer Coleman. He hesitate to respond knowing that there's no telling what might come out of Officer Simms mouth. After all he is a keeping it real kind of guy, no matter how it may come out.

"Um gone talk to Ms. Jones about getting a visitor up in here to talk to these kids about what really goes on behind those prison walls."

Officer Coleman was relieved that Officer Simms didn't say anything crazy or anything that had to do with a curse word.

"Yeah, you should talk to her about that and we will set it up. It will be worth a try," adds Officer Coleman.

Then suddenly a fart disrupted the meeting and the worse smell circulates thought out the dayroom. Without even thinking the boys move from that part of the room, as they fanned and covered their noses.

"Damn! Somebody funky," one boy called.

"Ole stinking booty out of control bowl movement face ass nigga," one resident says, as he quickly gets up moving away from the boy who broke wind.

The dayroom is suddenly filled with laughter!

"Damn, you stink." he adds holding his nose.

The other floor officers join in to assist giving the boys directives to go to their rooms for bed time. At this point, things gets just a little chaotic. The officers scramble to gain control of the residents. Some residents are talking to each other and others are running up and down the halls. They abruptly stop moving when they heard the sound of Officer Hill's whistle, "y'all better sit y'all ass down some damn where, before I shut this muthafucka down!"

The room got silent fast and control was regained. The residents thanked Office Coleman, Officer Simms and the other officers for sharing and giving them some good advice before going to bed.

CHAPTER 11

VISITATION

The following days seemed to drag by slower and slower. Bobby felt as though he was going to lose his mind. He was trying hard to stay head strong and keep his mind off of what was going on in the free world, but for some reason that was the most difficult thing to do; trying not think about the real world.

Most nights Bobby cried himself to sleep, day in and day out. But Anthony was a different story. It was as if Anthony was destined for jail. Often times it seemed like the juvenile detention center was just a home away from home.

Bobby stayed to himself, while his big brother Anthony was just the opposite. He was a busy body. He was always into something being loud causing trouble and disrespecting the officers.

Often times, Bobby would try to talk some sense into his brother's head but, Anthony was far too bullheaded to listen to his little brother. In fact, it seemed like he was only getting worse.

Once a week their mother would come to visit them. The visitation was a spectacle all by itself. Each week the visitation would be held in the gym. The floor officers would set up chairs in the gym, so the families could see their love ones. It was crazy to see the parents treat the juvenile's as though they had made some kind of big accomplishment; being in the detention center. I mean, the way most of these parents was acting you would have thought that their child had made the honor roll or something.

There was vending machines filled with soda, candy and all kind of junk food snacks. It was sad to see these parents reward these kids, as if they were saying great job for that armed robbery and other crimes. What kind of message were the parents sending to these already lost kids? At visitation everybody was smiling, happy and having a grand ole time like they was at a carnival. One other thing Bobby noticed was that there weren't many white kids in the detention center, but the ones that was there, their parents weren't playing that carnival bull crap. To the white parents this wasn't a game or a party. The white parents just seemed to have a different attitude about the situation, but Ms. Berry didn't play that either. No. Not at all. She was nice enough to her boys to get them something out the vending machine, but she didn't go way over board like most of the other parents did. She was more concerned with talking to her boys about their well-being and them becoming better young men.

The visits from his mother really helped Bobby deal with the things and the situation that he was going through. But at the same time, each time she came and she had to leave, made him feel like he was getting locked up all over again. He loved to see his mom come and it broke his heart every time she had to leave. For him, it wasn't getting any easier. He cried every time his mom had to leave.

As Bobby looked around, he could not understand how kids so young- who should have been free, could be having so much fun being locked up. Having all your freedom taking away wasn't fun for him at all.

Bobby also seen that the juvenile system really was like a revolving door. He seen the same group of boy's

come and go like it was a game. It was so bad that one boy got out of jail on Monday morning during breakfast and was back that same day for lunch. Is that crazy or what?

He thought that the worse thing about being locked up, was being away from his mom was Ms. Anne's cooking. The food in the Berry House was horrible he thought or maybe his mom was a really great cook. Chances are he was right. The food was really just that bad. He ate it any way, only because he really didn't have that big of choice. He ate just to survive. The worse thing was having to shower with 8 other boys every day and the J.D.O's (Juvenile Detention Officers) watching you as you showered.

Everyday Bobby was counting down the days until it was time for him to go home. Now, he understood what it meant when people said there's no place like home. During his stay away he tried hard not to think about home, but how are you not supposed to think about home. Maybe that was the problem with the majority of these kids. Maybe they didn't have a home he thought or maybe home was just a bad place for them.

As bad as it may sound for a lot of these kids, the detention center was home. Again it's sad to say, but in this place they had a roof over their heads and a bed to sleep in and a meal three times a day (They call that three hot's and a cot). A lot of the kids were on their own, on the streets with no place to go and no one to care for them. Some of their parents were on dope and crack, so bad that getting a high was more important than taking care of their own kids. It was this kind of situation that got many of these kids in trouble. Most of them was just trying to survive the best way they know how. Majority of the kids in the Berry House acted as though they had no home including Anthony. Bobby knew that Anthony had a home and he knew that he had love. So, why and how could he be so happy, so care free and was locked up? Not only was Anthony locked up, but to make matters worse, he was only 15 years old and he was facing grown man time. Bobby often wondered if Anthony even knew what he was really facing. Anthony was facing a murder by vehicle charge, even though it was an accident. It was still murder, which means poor Anthony wasn't going home anytime soon. This hurt Bobby and he had to find a way to deal with knowing that Anthony would be going away for at least 15 to 20 years or better.

At that point, Bobby decided not to hold anything against his brother. He decided to spend as much time with his brother as possible. He hoped that he could talk to his brother, so he could become a better young man.

The following days, Bobby began to attempt to talk to his older brother and it seemed as though it was useless. He was determined to see a better side of his brother. So, at every opportunity Bobby had, he talked to him. He soon became frustrated, because it seemed as though he couldn't reach him. Then one day, a strange thing happened, Anthony came to Bobby and told him that he had been doing a lot of thinking. He told him he was 15 and it was time for him to start taking a more responsible role. He said he was going to try to do better and start making better choices.

Anthony told Bobby, "I got you in this mess, so at least I can do for you is just start listening. I can try to become a better person, by putting God first, then me, then you and mom."

Bobby couldn't believe what his brother was saying to him, it seems as though after the many talks Bobby had with him, it was finally getting through to him. Or was Anthony just telling Bobby a bunch of fluff, fluff.

Bobby and Anthony started to hang out more during rec and leisure time. The two brothers began to spend even more time talking about God and many other things of importance. They also went to the many different programs that the detention center offered. Bobby could see after a while, that his brother's heart was in the right place.

Anthony really was sincere about making a change and becoming a better person. Sadly, it wasn't until then that he realized how serious the situation was and how deep of a ditch he had dug for himself. Gradually he begin to withdraw from the bad crowd. He was starting to sound like a change was occurring. He stopped cursing, getting into trouble and he even stop disrespecting the staff. Everyone took notice of the positive change, including the staff. When the JDO's told Anthony how well he had been doing, it made him feel very good about himself.

In a conversation that Bobby and Anthony had, Bobby asked his brother why he used to act out the

way he did. He was always talking about ditching school, smoking and stealing from people. Anthony told him that the reason why he always acted out was because, he felt like mom stopped loving him and giving him attention. Anthony told Bobby that he thought their mom loved Bobby more than him.

Anthony said, "it seemed like when I became a teenager she stopped giving me hugs and the attention she used to give him when I was young."

He went on to say, "it seemed like, the only time she knew I was there was when I was doing something bad. Other than that, it was like I didn't exist. She was always bragging about how smart you was and how proud she was of you. I wanted her to say those things about me," he told his younger brother. "She couldn't because I wasn't as half as smart as you." Then he lowered his head saying, "I guess I was jealous of you and her relationship."

Anthony wipes his face with the bottom of the t-shirt, as he kept trying to keep the tears from falling. Then he adds in a slumber voice, "that's the reason I started acting out. I just wanted mama's love and attention. That was the only way I knew how to get it."

Bobby sat there in total silence, shocked by what Anthony just revealed to him. He was just sitting there at a loss for words. He didn't know what to say or do, so he didn't say or do anything. He just placed his arm around his brother's and told him that he loved him and assured him that their mama loved him too.

CHAPTER 12

THE ESCAPE

On a bright sunny day, Bobby was on the rec yard talking to his brother when a new resident walked across to the rec yard. This resident just came in the night before, his name was John. He wasn't like the rest of the boys. No John was special. He was really special. He was funny and he was facing quite of bit of time. He was 16 years old from Morrow Georgia. (A small city South of Atlanta). He got himself caught up with some young adults who put him up to be the lookout guy while they robbed this liquor store, and when the job was over the guys dumped all the stolen guns off on him. He was crazy enough to let them.

After the robbery took place John went home and told his mother everything. He told her how these guys, who were supposed to be his friends, put him up to help rob this place and how they dropped the guns off on him after the robbery. After hearing this information, John's mother did what any concerned mom would do; she contacted the local police and reported the crime. So, now John is in the juvenile detention center awaiting the outcome. The young adults he was with was arrested and sent to the county jail.

While the three boys were talking, a loud whistle interrupted their conversation. The sound of the whistle was so loud the boys jumped, as to be startled.

"Ten-ten!" is called by the officers watching the residents on the rec yard to the control room.

Ten-ten is the code for fight: resident on resident assault. Officer Hill repeated in a loud demanding voice, "we need immediate medical assistant on the rec yard. Central, call 911, right now!" then he turned to the group of boys saying, "everybody line up!" he called directing the juveniles to line up.

Officer Simms followed in a panic state like voice weaving his hands yelling, "get in line!" trying to move the group of boys inside from the graphic gruesome scene.

Then the control room replied, "all staff to the rec yard. We have a ten-ten in progress. All available staff please report to the rec yard."

The officers became so excited, that they all panicked and called the wrong code, which should have been a "code blue." That's the code for medical emergency.

By now, all the residents present on the rec yard are starting to form a line as the officers directed. The residents have a hard time focusing for all the drama unfolding. They are concerned and confused by the gruesome site of Jamal, a juvenile who had received a 30 years for a murder. He lost the murder trial, some days before. Now, he is in the fight for his life, hanging on a fence in an attempt to escape.

His bloody body hangs from the top of the razor sharp fence. As he hangs on for dear life, he's experiencing excruciating pain. Words could not even begin to describe the pain he is feeling now. The boys looked at him in total shock, as they are told to line up to be moved from the rec yard area.

"Take the boys in and lock them all down!" ordered Officer Coleman, taking the leadership role as he often did as he ran over to help Jamal.

Officer Simms and Johnson conducted a quick emergency count. Then Officer Johnson calls the count into the central control.

"Ten-four.   40 male's from the rec yard to the dayroom unit," control replied.

"Ten-four," Officer Simms responded in somewhat of a panic.

Then he and the residents begin to head back to the dayroom. As the boys exit the rec yard, they turned their heads peering at Jamal, as he fought to hang on for dear life.

"Don't look back!" Officer Simms yells out, as he continued to shuffle the juveniles to a safe area. He was trying to keep the boys from looking at this horrific scene; however, they looked back at him as if they just knew that they would never see him alive again. Tears flowed like an endless river, from some of the boy's eyes. This was a heart breaking situation. Yet most of them just sucked it up and kept on moving, while others eyes were stuck on the injured boy.

Their friend was caught in the sharp razor bob wire trying to escape.   Helpless, by this time Jamal is bleeding like a fresh cut pig. From the looks of things, Jamal has severed a main artery. A huge pool of blood has dripped on the ground just below him.

As the residents are walking into the building the lieutenant alone with Mr. Boykin ran pass them in full speed, heading to the rec yard.   Both men were heading to the rec yard to assist.

 As the two men arrived, they are shocked at what their eyes behold.   They couldn't believe what they were witnessing.   Neither of them had never seen anything like it before. The director instantly felt sick to his stomach. Mr. Boykin clutched his stomach, as if he was going to throw up right there on the rec yard. Jamal was completely covered in blood from head to toe. It was unbearable to look at, hard on the stomach. They saw the large pool of blood dripping below the hanging boy. The blood was still flowing heavily, as if someone had turned on a blood faucet. Officer Simms had returned to the rec yard. Officer Hill was already there trying to keep the boy calm and keeping him from going into shock and passing out.

 It wasn't much either of them could do for him. By now, nine minutes had elapsed and things weren't looking good for Jamal. His breathing was heavy and slow, as if he was about to take his last breath. His eyes where blood shot red and rolled back in his head. He then went unconscious.

"Where is the damn ambulance?" Mr. Boykin asked, as he's looking back in the far distance and listening for sirens.

"Shit!" he added, turning back to the boy caught in the fence.

"Come on, just hang in their man. Help is on the way," Officer Simms says, looking up at Jamal from below trying to comfort him.

He is still bleeding profusely. Now, Officer Johnson is running back to the scene.

"The fucking ambulances haven't made it yet?" Officer Johnson says in an angry voice.

Officer Hill noticed that one of the razor sharp teeth of the wire point had pierced the side of his neck. The hole it created was small, but got bigger the more the boy moved. Just then the facility medical staff is seen in the distance running full speed to the scene. The medical staff has all kinds of equipment, including a stretcher and an oxygen tank.

"Somebody get a ladder and the first aid kit!" Mr. Boykin screamed.

"I copy that!" Officer Johnson responded, as he takes off in a mad dash. "I will bring some blankets," he yells out, as he sprints as fast as he could across the rec yard.

Finally, in the far distance there was the sound of the medical emergency team. The ambulance finally made it. It felt like this boy had been hanging up for hours.

"It's about damn time," Mr. Boykin said, looking into the distance.

In the distance, Officer Simms and Johnson is running across the rec yard, with their hands full on safety kit items. The officers along with the medical staff leaned the latter on the 20 feet fence. By this time, Jamal was shaking like a leaf on a tree on a fall wintery day. His clothing looked as though it had been through a paper shredder and his skin didn't look any better.

Officer Coleman and Officer Simms put on the protective gear and tried to put a grip on the razor sharp wire. He grabbed it from the emergency escape kit, which also had blue medical gloves, clear eye protective glasses and breathing mask. Officer Simms grabs the large wire cutter and began to cut the wire. By now, his body went limp. He is unconscious again. His breathing is slow and shallow.   Security and the medical staff see things aren't looking good at all.

The medical team immediately begins to take full control of the situation. The officers begin to move back, so the medical staff could render help to Jamal.

One of the paramedics quickly run over and began to give Jamal oxygen (using an oxygen mask), while another paramedic checked his vital signs. They were working hard to try and save his life. Jamal took a deep breath and opened his eyes, then his eyes rolled into the back of his head. His body became limp as he took his very last breath.

Everyone realized he was dead. It was over with. Blood was everywhere. It looked like several people were murdered, based on the amount of blood that soaked through his clothes. Blood was also on the ground and on the paramedic's clothes.   The paramedic put his hand on Jamal's face to close his eyes.

A huge rain cloud seemed to have stopped right above their heads. The wind began to blow very hard.

The thunder was so loud, everyone jumped with fright and looked at one another as to say, what do we need to do now?

They all knew at this point; it was nothing that nobody could do. They felt they needed to go inside before it started to rain. Officer Coleman said a prayer right there on the spot. The paramedics covered his body with a white sheet, and pulled out the stretcher and placed his bloody body on it.

The police arrive and gather information from the security staff and the paramedics. They roll out yellow tape that read, "DO NOT CROSS."

The atmosphere was gloomy. The feeling of unrest began to weigh heavily on the hearts and minds of everyone.

For several days after the attempted escape and death of Jamal, the atmosphere was different. Everyone was quiet, including the security staff. They all wondered, if there was something more they could have to done to save a human life. He was so young. He had his whole life ahead of him. For those who actually witnessed his death, they will never forget the horrific scene and the loss of life.

All they could say amongst themselves was, they don't want anything like this to ever happen again. They knew in their heart of hearts, they did the best they could to try to save his life. Bottom line, things just didn't turn out right.

Counseling was available for both the staff and the residents. The residents really needed counseling after what they had witnessed. They needed it more than the staff did. It was reported that some of the kids were having problems sleeping at night, after the traumatic event. Even the older kids began to have nightmares. This was a heart breaking time for everyone at the facility, but somehow they knew they would make it through.

Jamal was only 16 years old. He was a regular at the detention center. This time, he got sent to the Berry House for armed robbery, in which somebody was murdered. He had his day in court and got his sentenced to 30 years in prison. It was sad, his mother was on drugs real bad. He never knew his father. What makes matters worse, is the fact that Jamal had a baby 3 months ago.

One of Jamal's friend's said, that he had been acting real strange and talking crazy. He said he overheard him saying things like, "I can't go to prison and I ain't gone do no time. I can't! I will die first."

And of course his friend didn't take him serious. He never even told staff about what he was saying. His friends thought Jamal was just talking a whole lot of crap. Apparently he was serious and he had his mind made up about what he was going to do. He wasn't going to do 30 years for nobody. And as you know once someone makes up their mind, their mind is made up and that's it.

Many wondered, if Jamal was trying to kill himself or was he really trying to escape. I guess that's a question that nobody will ever know, but Jamal himself. In a way, I guess he did accomplish his goal because, now he is free, a free soul. He doesn't have to serve a day in prison. Rip Young J.

CHAPTER 13

THE MYTH

It wasn't long before things were back to normal. In this case, back to being a zoo. You know what I mean, boys cussing out to the officers and being disrespectful, threating to buck on staff and all that. Back to the wild and crazy days.

One day, while Bobby was at rec watching the other boys play football. He was having a conversation with two boys named Charles and Tim.

Charles was a quiet kid from the Atlanta area. He was telling Bobby and Tim this story about how the detention center was hunted.

Yeah right, Bobby thought. Then he asked Charles had he ever seen anything.

"Have I ever seen anything- like what?" Charles asked.

"Any super natural stuff... like a ghost?" Bobby asked.

"I'm confused. Are you asking if I've seen a ghost? Like a real ghost," Charles asked.

"Yeah."

"No. I never seen anything like that before, but I do believe this place is hunted?" he replied.

Bobby begins to say something then Tim asked, almost interrupting Bobby, "how do you know?" he asked.

Then the expression on Charles face changed like day and night. With a serious look on his face, he paused for a moment looking away from both boys. He then turned back to them and said, "my grandma used to work here. This was a long time ago, over 40 years ago."

Bobby and Tim's eyes grew big. The hair on the back of their necks stood up. Tim's mouth opened wide as did Bobby's.

"Are you serious?" Bobby asked, in disbelief.

"I'm not playing," Charles said, with that look of suspense.

Charles went on to tell them the unbelievable story how the state of Georgia bought the land back in the early 1940's. The land was dirt cheap, pennies on the dollar even. He also told them that the land used to be a grave yard for the county residents, that were welfare recipients who could not afford to pay to bury their love ones.

The state sold the land off, then a hospital was built for the mentally criminally insane, and then it was turned into the juvenile detention center after a mass murder happened at the hospital. They said over 12 people died in one night. The mental hospital is now the juvenile detention center.

Tim didn't know what to think. Bobby's jaw dropped as Charles spoke. Bobby couldn't believe what he was hearing. Charles told Bobby and Tim all about how the insane nurse came in to work one day and went on a shooting spree.

He still didn't know, if what Charles was saying was true. Bobby thought to himself, as he looked into the cloudless clear blue sky of the summer day, what if Charles is telling the truth. Could this really be an old grave yard underneath the Berry House? What if this place is hunted for real? What if this used to be a hospital for the crazy criminals?

Then more thoughts raced through Bobby's head, as he sat in the freshly cut grass. He had his back on the fence, with a piece of twig in his mouth looking like a good ole boy.

"Wait! There is more," Charles said, with a sign of suspense, "a nurse went crazy and killed everyone. But some people believe it was more to the story than what is being told. My grandma said it was really sad, then his voice dropped in tone as he said, "this place is hunted for real."

Bobby peered into the distance with intensity, recapping everything Charles just said. Then suddenly, Bobby snapped out of his thoughts and said to Charles, "um gone ask you again have you ever seen or heard anything weird around here?"

"No, I haven't," Charles replied.

"Okay, then I rest my case," Bobby said.

"You aint seen no ghost, cause there is no ghost.

Leave it alone man. Leave it alone," he added.

Just then, the officer blew his whistle and told Bobby to get off the fence. Bobby apologized and did as the officer instructed.

Charles didn't realize that when he was telling Bobby and Tim about the history of the place, Larry, Tony's home boy was sitting close by listening to everything he said. He didn't realize that Larry was ease dropping in on their conversation. The officer's yell, "rec time is over. Line it up!" The boy's did so and was escorted back to the unit.

The urban legend about the detention center was the county best well-kept secret. The residents had no idea about the story. The staff was aware of the events, but that's something they would rather not talk about.

As the word spread about the history of the center, the residents started asking questions. When they would ask specific questions about the history of the facility, the staff would never answered. They never said, yes it happened. They never said no, it didn't happen. They would always avoid the subject and the questions, as if it was taboo to talk about it.

The staff would always just play dumb about it. No one would say anything. Their lips were sealed, everybody except for Charles of course. Was Charles talking make believe or was he talking facts?

Now the word is spreading fast. Nothing was seen or heard that was crazy by the residents, but there was an exception. Randy would run around acting crazy, all the time. He would try to scare the mess out of the residents and staff, but he was just a joker. Other than that, everything seemed normal-for the most part.

The following day Larry couldn't wait to tell Tony and the rest of his loser crew what he overheard Charles talking about. Tony and his crew listened in total disbelief as Larry spilled the beans about Charles claim. Tony was really interested in the, so called urban legend and if Charles was really telling the truth. Tony just had to satisfy his curiosity.

The following day during rec time, Tony talked to Charles, "hey bruh, bruh come here for a minute."

Charles looked up and begins to walk in Tony's direction. To Charles this was odd indeed, because Tony never even so much as said what's up to him.

"I'll be right back," Charles said, to his friend looking back at them as he approached Tony.

"What's up?" Charles asked, looking at Tony and his crew.

What Charles was really thinking to himself was, what the fuck this nigga want? But of course he didn't say it. Tony was hanging out with his partners and they was bullying as usual.

"Shawty... was you telling people this place used to be a crazy house?" Tony asked, in a sarcastic voice.

Charles eyes grow big, as if he had been surprised. "It did!" he cried out, "this was a mental hospital before," he added.

"How the fuck you know that?" one of Tony's boys asked putting his two cents in.

"Man this nigga is lying like a muthafucka," another one added.

Tony and his crew begin to laugh at Charles, making him feel real embarrassed. "Wait!" Tony called out to his boys, while raising his hand, as to tell them to be quiet.

"What makes you think this used to be a crazy hospital?" Tony asked, waiting for an answer.

"My grandmother used to work here," Charles replied.

Then suddenly, Tony interrupted Charles, "where?"

"At this place when it was a hospital," Charles replied with all confidence that he was telling the truth, "she worked here when she was young –this was about 40 years ago," he added.

Tony and his boy's looked at Charles with that yeah right look on their faces. The boys aren't saying nothing. They were just listening to Tony drill Charles, as if he was some kind of investigator, "so, yo grandma told you all this?"

"No, I said. My grandma is dead, my mama told me this and my grandma told this to my mama," Charles said.

"Nigga please," Marcus says, busting out laughing. The others join in laughing at Charles.

The look of disappointment spreads across Charles face, "fuck y'all! I know what the fuck um talking bout," he says, throwing his hands up, as he turns from the group of meddling boys.

"And this place is haunted!" Charles yells back at the boys.

"Have you seen a ghost muthafucka? This place aint no muthafuckin haunted nigga!" one of the boy's fires back as Charles walks away.

"Yo ass just crazy!" another one adds, trying to show out in front of the leader; Tony the bad boy.

"Lame as nigga," Charles whispered underneath his breath, looking back at the boys still laughing and making fun of him.

Charles was upset because, he felt that no one believed him, and Tony and his friends made a fool out of him. Charles has his mind made up, and he was sticking to his story. He thought to himself why would my mom lie about something like that?

As far as Tony went he didn't believe Charles, no not one bit. But something deep inside him said, that maybe ole Charles had some truth to this crazy outlandish story. Tony didn't know what part may have been true, but he felt he just had to find out. They say that curiosity killed the cat and it was definitely getting the best of Tony. He had to find out what really went on. He had to satisfy his curiosity, if that was the last thing he did. So, what did Tony do? He advised a plan and put it into full effect.

Later that same day, Tony asked Officer Johnson if he could help with the cleaning of the dining room. Officer Johnson agreed. After dinner time was over Tony, Marcus and Officer Johnson began there cleaning detail.

By now, you should know that Officer Johnson is always catering to bad boy Tony. Always giving him anything that he asked for, as if he owned Tony a favor or something.

When dinner was over the rest of the males was instructed to line up and was escorted back to the male unit, with the exception of Tony and Marcus. They both stayed back to help out with the cleaning detail. Once on the unit, all the boys were locked down and the officers started the shower process.

Meanwhile, back in the dining area, Marcus and Tony has started there cleaning with Officer Johnson. "We need some more cleaning supplies," said Marcus.

Officer Johnson and the boys go back to the unit to get more supplies. Together they gathered the mop, broom, chemicals and the unit cleaning cart. Then, they returned to the dining area where they resumed their cleaning detail.

While Tony begins to clean, his mind begins to wonder about the conversation that took place earlier with Charles. Tony tries hard to not think about it, but the harder he tries to put in the back of his mind, the more thoughts kept popping up in his head. It was like the thoughts wouldn't go away. He just had to know the truth. After a while, he decided to ask Officer Johnson about the infamous, so called urban legend.

Tony just knew that if Officer Johnson knew anything, he would tell him everything. And heck, why not? He tells Tony everything else. While cleaning, Tony decided to strike up a conversation with Officer Johnson about his favorite football team which happened to be the Atlanta Falcons. After about 10 minutes of small talk, Tony suddenly paused and then look of confusion came across his face. You know that strange look, like when someone want to ask you something or the look like someone want tell you something. Yeah that look. Tony just looked at Officer Johnson in silence.

"What nigga?" Officer Johnson exclaimed, raising his hands as he shrugs his shoulders.

"I want to ask you about something," Tony replied, looking directly into Officer Johnson eyes.

All the while, Marcus is still sweeping the floor on the other side of the room, not paying much attention to the others listening to his headphones. He seemed to be having the time of his life all by himself.

Tony finally got up the nerves to ask Officer Johnson what he wanted to know. "What did this place used to be before it was a jail?"

"First of all this ain't no jail, this a damn daycare for bad ass boys like you," Officer Johnson replied with a slight grind on his face trying to avoid the boy's question.

"You know what um talking about. Stop playing dumb. Nall, you ain't playing yo ass is just dumb for real." The two laugh.

"No for real, what did this place used to be a long time ago?"

Tony begins to see that Officer Johnson is trying hard to avoid his question and is avoiding direct eye contact with him, while he is talking about the history of the building. This only makes make Tony even more suspicious. Now, he wants to dig deeper.

"Damn you noisy! Why you asking me all these damn questions, that I don't know shit about. Do I look like um two hundreds year old lil nigga?"

"Hell yeah," Tony replied. They both laugh.

Just then Tony looked up and seen Lt. Wayne passing by from the administration area.

"Let me go and holla at Lt. Wayne right quick," Tony asked while dropping his broom and walking out the door even before the Officer Johnson can give him permission. He was trying to catch the Lieutenant before entered into the admin door.

"Yeah it's okay," Officer Johnson said.

"I will be right back," he said rushing out the dining area.

Tony then runs over to Lt. Wayne in the multipurpose area.

"Hey what's up Tony? How are you doing?" Lt. Wayne asked.

"Um cool," Tony said, "um...can I ask you a question Lt?"

"Sure. What's on yo mind?" Lt. Wayne says with a big smile.

"Well... umm, I want to know what did this place used to be a long time ago."

Lt. Wayne looks at the boy, as if he was thinking to his self, what in the hell is this boy talking about. Lt. Wayne had a very funny look on his face with a funky fake smile to go with it.

"Well, um not sure what this place used to be," then he paused, "why you ask me that?"

"Well, Charles. Do you know who Charles is?"

"Yeah, I think I do. Who he is? You talking about the real quit one?" Lt. Wayne asked.

"Yes, that's him. Charles said that his grandmother used to work here and she told him that this used to be a mental hospital. Is that true Lt?" Tony asked, looking into Lt. Wayne eyes.

Lt. Wayne looked somewhat baffled of the question. He begins to stutter, as if he was trying to think quick on his feet.

"Is this place hunted?"

Lt. Wayne gave Tony another fake smile, "ain't no ghost up in here. Have you ever seen one in here?" Lt. Wayne asked the young boy.

"No sir, I haven't," Tony replied.

"Who told you all this crazy stuff anyway?"

Lieutenant asked, reaching for a pen and a note pad out of his back pocket.

"Charles. I told you that," Tony said.

Lt. Wayne begins to write in his note pad. Tony thanked Lt. Wayne for speaking with him and returned to the dining area where Marcus was finishing mopping the floor.

The following Monday morning, Lt. Wayne went into Mr. Boykin's office and told him all about how Tony was asking questions about the history of the building, and also what Charles told them what his grandma said. He claimed, she used to work here a long time ago. He told Mr. Boykin that Tony was asking about this place being hunted and some stuff about a grave yard.

Mr. Boykin became angry at once. "I want Tony ass up here right now!" Mr. Boykin fired back pointing his index finger downward.

"No-no, it wasn't Tony who said all this stuff, it was Charles." He said, trying not to confuse Mr. Boykin.

"It was Charles who said all this to Tony," Lt. Wayne begin to explain.

"Who the hell is Charles?"

"He is the one who told all this to Tony." Lt. Wayne relied.

"I want him in my fucking office, now!" he said directing his anger toward the lieutenant.

"Okay- I will go get him right now."

Lt. Wayne quickly exits Mr. Boykin's office, on his way to the unit to get Charles.

Mr. Boykin was very disturbed to know that one of his residents was spreading rumors about his facility.

He was even more upset because someone was telling rumors about things that happed a long time ago. But, if it was in fact just a crazy rumor why would Mr. Boykin be so angry. Why would he be so mad and further more why would he even care if it was just a rumor. Maybe, because Charles wasn't just spreading rumors, maybe just maybe he was telling the truth.

  After about ten minutes went by, Lt. Wayne returned with Charles. The boy looked a little uneasy and definitely confused, as if he didn't know why he was in Mr. Boykin's office.

"Come in and have a seat," Mr. Boykin ordered standing behind his desk starring down at Charles like a judge or something.

"Step out for just a moment," Mr. Boykin order to Lt. Wayne in a calm yet threating tone.

"Yes sir," he replied slipping out the door, shutting it softly, behind him.

Charles sat in the chair in front of Mr. Boykin's large cherry oak desk.

  "You doing okay son?"

"Yes sir. How are you?" Charles said, as his voice cracks like an out of tune instrument.

Mr. Boykin didn't respond, he just gave Charles this stare, then he put both elbows on his desk with fingers enter locked, leaning slightly forward in his big leather chair.

"Son, what do you know about this place?" Mr. Boykin asked, with his eyes locked on Charles eyes.

"Well... um, I know the rules in the resident hand book and I know the dayroom rules. I."

Before the boy could get his next word out, Mr. Boykin abruptly interrupted him.

"No. Um not talking about that bullshit. What do you really know about this place?" Then, Mr. Boykin's voice drop to a whisper tone, "um talking about the history of this place." His eyes were still locked on Charles like a bullet proof safe.

"Oh yeah," Charles said. As if he was surprised, but yet relieved that was all Mr. Boykin wanted to talk about. Finally, he thought, someone wanted to hear about what he knew.

"My mama told me that my grandma told her, about how she used to work here and she said that this place used to a mental institution. She also told my mama that one of the nurses went crazy. He was a man. He killed like 12 or 13 people," he said with an innocent expression on his face.

Mr. Boykin leaned back in his seat with a stone cold look upon his face. He wasn't happy about what he was hearing, but he just let Charles talk as he listened. Mr. Boykin begins to frown, as he leaned forward in his chair.

"What else did yo mama tell you?" he asked with a straight face and a stern tone.

Charles could see that Mr. Boykin was becoming upset. He then took a deep breath, as to get his thoughts together. As this man stairs at him like an angry judge, Charles begin to feel uneasy about this meeting.

"My mom said... she said my grandma told her this was a grave yard before and this place was a hospital."

"Listen boy!" Mr. Boykin said, loudly and abrupt as he stands up behind his desk. Now Charles knows that

Mr. Boykin is angry, as he sinks into his seat. The boy was scared and didn't know what to say or do.

"I don't care who told you all this crazy bullshit, but it's all lies and nothing but lies. All that shit yo mama told you is a lie and I bet not never hear you repeat that shit to nobody else."

Then he leaned over the desk getting closer to Charles face. As he did the boy leaned back too, "but it is true Mr. Boykin," said Charles in a shaking voice.

"Do you understand and hear what the hell um saying to you boy!"

"Yes sir... I understand," Charles answered, as the tears slip down his cheeks.

By this time, Charles is visibly shaken. Then, Mr. Boykin flops himself back into his chair, as he takes a deep breath, he looks out the window of his office. He then turns back to Charles.

"If I ever hear another word about this place being hunted or any other crazy bullshit, um going to ship yo little ass, so far away that if and when yo damn mama see you, she won't even recognize yo ass. AM I FUCKING CLEAR!" he said, in a yelling tone.

"Yes sir," he says, as he lowered his head and wipes his tears away.

"NOW GET THE FUCK OUT MY OFFICE!"

With tears in his eyes, Charles slowly stood up and as he reached for the door, Lt. Wayne's face appeared. Apparently, Lt. Wayne had been at the door listening the whole time.

No doubt about it, Mr. Boykin had broken Charles down. Not only did he hurt his feelings, he also hurt his pride as well. That was the end of that. Charles never spoke of the facility history ever again.

CHAPTER 14

360

For the time being, Bobby is doing a lot better for the most part. His mother has been coming to visit him on a regular basis, and just that alone keeps him strong and focused. After all, Bobby is just buying time at this point, because he knows he will be going home real soon. It is his brother that he is truly worried about. But Anthony has made a 360 positive turn around. He is becoming a new person and in Bobby eye's that is definitely is a good thing for him.

The fact that Anthony has made such improvement really makes Bobby sad for the fact that his older brother and he had to get locked up together in order to become close.

It's a shame that it took Anthony to catch a case and to lose his freedom to find himself. Why did it have to come to this Bobby sat and wondered? Bobby couldn't understand why all this had to happen to him and his brother.

He could always hear his mother's voice just as clear as a bell in the distance saying, "everything happens for a reason, don't never question God."

And although many times he wanted to question God, he never did.   Bobby begins to enjoy the little festivities that the detention center offered.   He started playing sports during recreation time and he even started to go to all the social activities; like church and the self-development classes. He was also hanging out a lot with Eddy which he really enjoyed his company. Eddy made Bobby laugh all the time. He was always saying something funny or doing something crazy.

Bobby and Charles had also become real good friends, but all the sudden Charles started to act weird, somewhat a bit strange. Charles wasn't acting like his normal self. He wasn't joking like he used to or talking as much. Things was just different with him.

Bobby didn't know why, but for reason Charles wasn't the same. Before, Bobby and Charles talked about any and everything. Charles never told Bobby or anyone else about what took place in Mr. Boykin's office that day and this was probably why Charles was acting this way, so different. But nevertheless, all and all it was the same thing boys fighting and acting crazy. Every day Bobby saw a new black face. The same people coming and going like it was some kind of joke. Bobby just decided on two things, one-to do his time like a man and two- like his brother told him, "you know you going home soon, just spend this time with me, while he have the time together."

His older brother would often remind him, that he was going to be gone for a long time and to make the best of his situation and any other situation he may find himself in.

Bobby was quite surprised to hear such wisdom coming from his brother's mouth. He was proud of Anthony's change. In fact, he hadn't been in any trouble and even has walked away from several fights. Bobby thought that Anthony felt guilty for getting him into all this mess. So, in his mind, he felt Anthony was changing more for him, than for his own self. He didn't care what the reason was, he was just happy to see his big bro doing so well.

CHAPTER 15

THE VISIT- SIR TOO THUGGISH

The following day, the residents were told that, if they behaved well, they had a special visitor coming to see them during leisure time. All day long the boys were sure to be on their best behavior, so that they could get the special visit. All day long whispers filled the atmosphere about who the special visitor would be. Some speculated that it would be Atlanta's own, "Ace 1" a well-known rapper while others said that it might be Atlanta's famed producer, "Ticking Tone." Whoever it is, the residents were on their very best and they all were excited.

During leisure time the group is gathered and seated in the dayroom. The room is filled with excitement and anticipation about the expecting guess.

"Alright everyone," Officer Coleman says, as he stands before the group of young boys with their eyes wide open full of anticipation. "I know you all are ready for your special guest." The boys were so excited that some of them could not sit still. "So, with

no further ado, boys please welcome Toe

Joe," Officer Coleman says, as he led the group of boy's eyes towards the entrance door of the unit.

Mumbling quickly filled the dayroom, as the boys all turned around to see who would be walking through the door. Some mumbled, "who the hell is Toe Joe?"

Of course, none of them never ever even heard of the name, Toe Joe before. So needless to say, when they didn't see a famous face they were highly disappointed. The smiles quickly turned to frowns. Suddenly everybody had that W.T.F. look on their face.

Toe Joe slowly entered the dayroom draped in a one piece bright orange jumpsuit. He was accompanied by two other white gentlemen, which both was wearing matching blue and gray uniforms and hats that read Robinson Corrections on the sleeve and on the their caps.

Toe Joe stood about 6'5" and was BLACK. I mean BBLLAACCKK, um talking about that lights out BLACK with a baldhead. He weighed about 235 or 240. He was nothing but muscles. When he walked in he was already sweating. He didn't have no gym muscles, no um talking about straight home grown prison muscles. There is a difference, trust me. This dude's muscles had muscles.

As Toe Joe walks to the front of the group, the Juvenile officers moved towards the back of the room. Toe Joe's leg irons drag across the dayroom floor, as he makes his way to the front. The sounds on the chains echoed off the walls and throughout the room. The residents gasped, as their eyes widen with look of amazement by this man stature and physic.

Toe Joe was a huge jolly green giant type dude, but he wasn't jolly at all. He was big and a very dark skinned man, in fact he was so dark he was close to purple. If someone was to cut off the lights, Toe Joe would have disappeared. It would have been an attempt to escape declared.

The skin on his hands was thick, rough and tough. His hands were rough enough to start a fire, if he rubbed them together. I mean you could strike a match in the palms of his hands. This man's arms and neck was filled with prison tattoos. This guy looked like he haven't ever been free. He looked like he had been born in a prison. Toe Joe looked like, every day was a bad day.

This huge black man stood tall and bold before the group of boys, his eyes were as red as fire. His eyes held a cold heart less stare, as if there was no soul

behind the blood shot eyes. He looked like he was ready to go crazy at any minute and the residents eyes were fixed on him like they were frozen in time.

As the correction officers took the off the chains, the sound echoed as the chains hit the floor. The boys cringed and jumped to the loud sound. The boys felt intimidated at the demeanor of this hardcore prison inmate. This man was cut up like a bad check.

He stood up in front of them, with this heartless heavy stare gazing across the dayroom at the youngsters. His presence was strong, heavy and dangerous. The group stared back into his empty eyes with a look fear and terror in their eyes. They were quiet, so quiet that you could hear a mice piss on the carpet. Now that's quiet. His look was cold. You could tell he had been broken by life. This man had an animal like instinct and he wasn't there to play no games with nobody. This man was the next thing to a beast.

"What's up youngsters?" he spoke in a deep thunderous voice. His red eyes pierced through the group of boys like a laser beam. If looks could kill, every one of these kids would have been dead as a door knob. Then he paused for a moment, he looked

at each boy from front to back and side to side. "Man it hurt me to know where y'all life is headed," he said using broken English.

"Y'all just don't know the life y'all is creating for y'all self. You see... I was young and dumb just like yous. When I was young couldn't nobody tell me shit-my fault officer," he says throwing his hand up, as to apologize to the officers for cursing. "See-when I was young, I was in and out of places like this all the time. Y'all got the game messed up. Y'all think this is all fun and games but it's not. This is y'all life and you throwing it all away. I see they got y'all the BET, cable TV and all these other games. Hell, y'all think y'all is at home. For some of y'all this is better than home. I see they even got y'all a play station. What y'all don't know is that all y'all getting pimped and played, and y'all don't even know it," he says, as he paused and looked across the room. The young group of boys looks back at him in suspense.

"Yeah the system is the pimp and y'all is the little hoe's," he says as he started to look down slowly pacing the floor.

"The system wants you!" he proclaimed, "do you think they want you to go to school and become

successful?" Some boys knobbed their heads as to agree.

"Hell nall!" he says in an angry voice, as he makes a motion with his right hand.

"They got y'all right where they want you, locked up with no place to go and no hope. They got this game on lock -hell they the ones who made this lock up B.S. and you all so dumb y'all playing right into it. Just like I did. Now, who wants to do time like me?" he asked the group, as he paused, "y'all are the selected few that society has already gave up on. So, now y'all is just a number. Y'all don't know that yet-do you? They not gone tell y'all this bit of info because they got to keep them beds full."

Then, Toe Joe paused for a moment, as if a fresh idea had come to his mind, then he proceeded with a question for the group.

"Do anybody know how much money they are making off of you all each day? Anybody know?"

The residents look at each other as to look for an answer. No one replied.

"Well, I will tell you, 500 dollars a day. Now y'all look around and tell me how many 500 dollars is in here right now. I see a hell of a lot. And you know how much it cost the state to feed, clothe, and house you all each day?"

Toe Joe paused again waiting for an answer. "Two dollars and twenty five cents a day. Now you do the math. And y'all in here thinking y'all ain't getting pimped. Yeah, they pimping y'all hard and heavy, big-time. Y'all young asses better wake up fast. Don't feel bad cause um getting pimped too, even harder than you. I dun already pimped over twenty years of my life away. What um trying to tell y'all is, this is no game. They got all these games and fun stuff for you all to keep ya mind off what's really important and that's getting ya life back together once you get out this place –this system... It's hard to get out and um telling you all, anything you do they gone violate you and send you right back here until they can send you up the road to prison-and that's the real deal-potna..."

For a moment dead silence falls upon the room.

"Who gone protect you, if you go to prison... NO BODY!" he yells.

"You can't call for no officer to help you and you shoal can't call for yo mama- because it ain't nothing she or anybody else can do to help you.   You just S.O.L. Everyday somebody getting raped, stabbed or killed. This is every day. It's a concrete jungle, it ain't no bull crap.

"Understand and know this- they just getting y'all ready for the next level and y'all don't even know what the next level is.   Um talking about the penitentiary. Just like around Thanksgiving when they started feeding them turkeys and getting them fat, they getting them fat for a reason, for the slaughter and putting them on your Thanksgiving table. We'll that's the same with you. They getting y'all fat and ready for the penitentiary. Straight up. I want you to take a look at yourselves. What do you see the most of?" he asked the group of young boys.

"Turn and look around, all I see is a bunch of us. Right now this facility is 95% black that's in here right now. I see a few Mexicans and two or three white kids, but this is how it is all across America. A whole lot of Mexicans and blacks are locked up, young and old. This is happening nationwide, from state to state. To make matters worse is the fact that, you all think

going to jail and getting locked up is cool. Y'all think y'all is hard as hell in jail, I don't get it."

Then, Toe Joe raised his voice saying, "man this crap ain't cool. This ain't nothing but modern day slavery! And y'all lil niggas aint hard. Yeah-all the man did was change the game up. They traded the chains for these bars. Instead of lynching, they using T.I.M.E that's time. They hanging us with 10, 20, and 30 years or better. That's the new lynching game. It's all the same game mane. Y'all running around here thinking this crap is cool. Y'all throwing all your opportunities away. Y'all throwing your education away! Y'all throwing time away! Time you could never get back, because y'all locked up. This may not be for all y'all, as a matter of fact, this aint for everybody cause some of y'all want to be just like me. Um talking to the ones that wants to be somebody in life. Um talking to the ones that value their freedom and the ones who want a nice family with a wife and some kids. That's the one um talking to. If you want my life, you don't got to listen, just keep doing what you doing, you on the right path. A fast path to nowhere and a path to destruction. If your tired of being told what to do and when to go to bed um talking to you. If your tired of wearing other people's funky draws. Um talking to

you. If I don't do nothing but reach one person, then me coming here was worth it. For the ones that feel where um coming from, when you go back to the block don't glamorize this lock down stuff. Talk to the lil homies and let them know what's really going on."

Then we want on to tell the boy's, "you can be anything that you want to be. It all boils down to the choices you make and the life you want to live."

As the officers walk up to Toe Joe, he is instructed to turn around and face the wall. The hand cuffs and legs irons are placed back on him. As he exits, the dayroom remained quiet. Even after he was gone, it was as if you could still feel his heavy presence.

CHAPTER 16

THE DISCOVERY OF

A few days has passed, since Charles told Tony some crazy stores about the detention center. Tony still wasn't sure about what Charles had told him some days ago, but one thing was for certain; Tony could see that when he asked the staff about the urban legend both Lt. Wayne and Officer Johnson acted real strange, especially being that Officer Johnson told him everything.

The thought of the truth just wouldn't escape his mind. All he knew is that he had to get to the bottom of things. He needed to know the truth. He just couldn't rest otherwise. So what did Tony do?

Tony devised a plan to dig deep, so that the truth could be uncovered. So, one day, Tony talked Officer Johnson into letting him and his boys clean up the gym. Once they finished, Tony asked could they clean the administration area. Officer Johnson told the crew that area was restricted and they weren't allowed to be in the area for any reason. Tony being Tony wasn't trying to hear that noise Officer Johnson was talking. His mind was made up. He was going to find out the truth, if that was the last thing he did. So, Tony kept pressuring Officer Johnson until he finally gave into his request.

With cleaning cart already loaded, Officer Johnson looks both ways to make sure the coast was clear, since no one appears to be in sight Officer Johnson and the boys quietly sneak through the door of the restricted area.   Once inside the restricted administration area, Officer Johnson looked at each of the boys making eye contact and told them not to tell a single soul. Of course the boys agreed but never the less Tony and crew had their own hidden agenda.

The boys begin to clean the admin area. After about twenty minutes Officer Johnson is laughing and joking with them and before long he begins to let his guard down. Tony asked Officer Johnson for permission to use the bathroom which was just down the hall. Officer Johnson gives him the okay, as well as the directions.

Meanwhile, the boys and Officer Johnson are talking about sports and having themselves a grand ole time. This was just a diversion to keep the officer distracted. While Officer Johnson is being played like a sucker mc, Tony has walked into the men's bathroom and posted up for about 3 or 4 minutes before slipping into the record's keeping department just down the hall.

While Tony is in the records room fumbling around for information, Larry shows up. Now there are two of them in the record keeping room. Larry tells Tony that the coast is clear. He also tells him that Marcus and Patrick were keeping Officer Johnson busy. The two boys continue to look around in the dim of the light. The boys are nervous, their heads are sweating profusely. Their hearts are beating over, 100 beats per seconds. They both know that if they get caught in this area Officer Johnson could lose his job and they could very well get some additional charges; which could lead to more time in juvenile hall.

Suddenly, Tony found a set of keys, lying on the table next to a desk. There was also a file cabinet that read in big bold letters, "CONFIDENTAL. DO NOT OPEN!" Tony took the set of keys and began to try each key to open the file cabinet. "Fuck!" Tony said, as he tried each key.

None of the keys seemed to fit, then all the sudden, he slid the key into the key hole. And with the turn of the key and like magic the confidential drawer door slid open.

Meanwhile, the other boys are up front still trying to keep Officer Johnson distracted. Tony and Larry had been gone for some time now and Officer Johnson is starting to feel a little uneasy. He senses something is not right, as he repeatedly glances at his watch, looking down the hall for any sign of Tony and Larry.

As Tony slowly slid the "CLASSIFIED FILE" out of the file cabinet, they both are breathing heavy and their eyes are big and full with anticipation about what they about to find out.

Tony opens the folder slowly and carefully, as if it was the grand old book of life. Once the folder was open the boys receive the shock of their lives and they really weren't ready for this kind of information. Their eyes quenched as they read the papers in the file. As the two boys read paper after paper they both glance at one another with their mouths wide open in disbelief. The rumors, the urban legends, the tall tells. Well, come to find out according to the legal documents it was all true. This wasn't something somebody just said. No. Now, Tony has the black and white, um talking about documentation.

In the confidential folder, it stated that the building was a mental institution. As Tony and Larry look further they come across some old newspaper clippings. The boys begin to read each clipping, one by one. One headline read, "12 PATIENTS MURDERD DURING DISGRUNTLE NURSE RAMPAGE." Another read, "ONE COMMITS SUICIDE AFTER MURDEROUS KILLING SPREE AT LOCAL MENTAL HOSPITAL."

The boys look at one another in total disbelief. They are both shocked to the core. The headlines continued about the mass murders and the closing of the facility. Tony felt as though he had seen as much as he wanted to see, just as he was closing the flies, a piece of document fell out of the folder. Tony picked up the document, which was even more shocking information. It told how the state of Georgia purchased the land for cheap, at a state surplus auction and the fact that the land was once a burial site for the county residents. The document said the land was bought for pennies on the dollar back in the early 1930's. But several years later it become a mental institute.

The boy's knees just about buckled. Now that they know, this new information they became frighten of what they may see or hear. They were scared off their rockers. Suddenly the door slammed. Then there is talking in the distance.

"You hear that?" Tony asked Larry. He was shaking and his eyes as big as silver dollars, with trembling in his voice.

Then he paused and peeked his head out of the records room, then turned back to Larry and says, "man! now, I wish we hadn't found all this information."

"I know. That's that bullshit," Larry responds, "we got to get the fuck out of here," he adds.

"Let's go!" Tony quickly advised. " Let's put all this shit back first," he cried out picking up the papers placing them back into the folder.

Tony and Larry could hear the voices getting closer and closer. After putting everything back, both boys quickly shut the door to the records room and darted back into the restroom without being detected. Just then Officer Johnson appeared in the hall way with the other two mischievous boys. Tony and Larry come out the bathroom acting calm and cool as though nothing ever happened

"Where the hell y'all been for the last damn 6 hours?" Officer Johnson said, asking sarcastically." He looks around, "y'all ass was probably in some shit."

Then, he walks over to the records door and pulls on the handle. The door is secured. The two boys look at one another as to say close call. He thanks the boys for helping him clean and escorted them back on the unit.

That night, terrifying images danced in Tony's and Larry's heads about what they had discovered. They both stayed up all night looking up at ceiling and jumping out their skin, every time they heard a bump or seen a shadow. They couldn't wait for the next morning, so they could come out their rooms to tell about what they had found.

Now, the urban legend wasn't just a legend at all. It wasn't just a tall tell, it wasn't just a myth, but it was a fact. Turns out that everything that Charles said was true and that was the reason why Mr. Boykin was so pissed off. It was all there in black and white. It was all true!

CHAPTER 17

COUNTING DOWN

Several weeks later, Bobby was showing a glow with a smile of freedom. He realize that with each and every passing day he was one step closer to being a free soul. A free person. A free young man. With each passing day, all he could think about was going home and sleeping in his own bed, in his own room and wearing his own clothes. He also thought about spending time with his mother he missed so dearly.

Every day that's all he talked about was going home. Bobby was very excited to be leaving soon and in some kind of odd way when he thought about, it he was sad in some strange way. He was actually appreciative of his crazy experience. It made him tough. It made him to appreciate every little thing that life had to offer and not to take freedom nor life for granted. Although Bobby was young he was also very wise.

Bobby felt that being locked up made him more aware of his surroundings, he seemed to have gathered a whole new outlook on everything in life in general. He appreciated even the smallest, the simple things like just breathing fresh air and just being free to go and do the things he love to do.

Like the man that came to the center from the prison said, "sometimes you don't know how good you got it just to be free."

After several months of being locked up with a bunch of boys acting like wild animals, he felt like he could relate to Toe Joe and the other people that came to speak to him and the other boys.

From time to time, his mind drifted back on Rudy. Sometimes he would just laugh when he thought about some of the things that came out of his mouth. He thought about how Rudy protected him and about that time when he beat the crap out of Tony and his crew.

Rudy was a true friend. The kind of guy that would give you his last, but then again he was that same guy that would also take your last.

He wondered why, so many black young men seem to have been marked a three times losers from the start. People like Rudy for instance; he wasn't really a bad person, not at all. He had just been dealt some bad cards, he thought. What else can a person do when they are 10, 11 or 12 years old? No one to teach them the right way. No one to encourage them. No one to show them values, respect and love. These are the young people that society has thrown away and are forgetting about. No longer a human, just a throw away-reduced to a faceless number and a nameless body. How can you win when society has already determined you a loser? How can you love when your environment is comprised of hate and raging anger?

Bobby's heart went out for people like Rudy. Yes, these people are criminals, but we forget they are humans first. Humans with a heartbeat and humans with minds and souls. He really missed his friend.

As happy as he was to be leaving the detention center soon, the thought of Anthony not coming home broke his heart. Anthony was his only brother and in a sense, he was all he had besides his mom. He was really hurt that his big brother had to go to prison, not just that, he was going to be going away for a long time. 10 years or longer.

Man that's a long time he thought. He had only been locked up for a couple of months, but it seems like eternity. Just the thought of that time, ten years or more, just about made him sick to his stomach. He felt helpless because there was nothing that he could do except pray for his brother and try to be strong for him and his mom.

As Bobby looked around the dayroom, he noticed that majority of the boys seemed to be heading for the big trap, and he didn't understand why these kids didn't get the bigger picture. There was always someone taking out the time to talk to these kids, but it seem like these kids thought it was cool to be locked up. It was like jail was home and home was jail.

For the life of Bobby he couldn't understand it.

If I had a nickel for every kid that came to jail I would be a millionaire, he thought.

CHAPTER 18

ANTHONY HAS HIS DAY

One day, during leisure time Bobby is in the dayroom enjoying a movie with the rest of the boys. Anthony is setting across the room playing a quiet game of cards- maybe 21, as most residents love to play. Officer Coleman walks over to Anthony and whispers something into his ear. He stood up and the two of them walked down the hall into Anthony's room. After about five to six minutes Bobby saw the two of them walking back up the hall. Bobby notices that Anthony has some items in his hands, but he didn't pay it much attention. He did notice Anthony walking slowly with his head down. He appears to be really sad, as if something was wrong.

As he walked past Bobby, Anthony give his brother a nod as to say what's up with a head motion, he then says, "all right then lil bruh. Hold it down man."

The boy setting next Bobby was watching Anthony and Officer Coleman. The boy sees that two other officers are putting hand cuffs on him. The boy then turns to Bobby and whispers quietly into Bobby's ear, "hey bruh... I think Anthony is leaving."

"What?" Bobby replied brushing the boy off.

"Bobby! they taking Anthony off. Look bruh!"

This of course gets Bobby attention and fast.

"What?"

Bobby quickly turned around looking towards the multi-purpose area where he sees Anthony being handed cuffed. He then saw the other two officers who had on black jackets with white letters that read, "Stonewall JDC."

Anthony was now leaving Bobby within the system. All they had was each other, now they are being separated. At the site of this, Bobby got up to get a closer look at what was going on. The officers directed Bobby to sit down, but he ignored the officers and continued to walk out the dayroom into the multi-purpose area where his brother was.

Bobby walked over to the two officers who had just finished cuffing Anthony and asked, "where is my brother going?"

"He's being transferred," the transport officer said, in a rude tone.

Just then the officers from the dayroom arrive to the area. Anthony is shackled up looking at Bobby with tears running down his face. His head was down like he was trying to hide the falling tears.

When Bobby saw his brother crying, he begins to cry too. He pats his older brother on the back to comfort him. Telling him that everything was going to be alright.

"Your brother is going to be alright," Officer Coleman said, in a calm tone, as if he was about to cry himself.

"Please don't take my brother away," Bobby cried to the transportation officers.

Anthony slowly turns to his brother to tell him to be strong and everything was going to be all right. Bobby begins to plead with Officer Coleman and the others. Just then Officer Simms appeared in the doorway of the dayroom. He took notice of Bobby crying as he begins to throw a fit.

"Bobby! Bobby!" Officer Simms yells out.

It was like Bobby couldn't hear him at all. He is still pleading to the officers about his brother. Officer Simms, Coleman and others attempt to grab Bobby to get him under control. Officer Parker then comes over to assist with the situation. By this time, all the officers are trying to get Bobby back to the unit. By now, Bobby is totally out of control, screaming, kicking and fighting all the while Anthony is yelling to his brother to stop fighting, trying to calm him down.

The transporting officers begin to move Anthony to the intake area. Anthony yells out, "love you lil bruh!" before he disappears through the doors leading to intake area.

The officers have a difficult time trying to control Bobby and getting him to calm down. The staff had to drag him from the multi-purpose area through the dayroom all the way to his room. The other residents watched in terror as he passed through the dayroom fighting, kicking and screaming. He fought and cried all the way to his room. By the time he got to his room, it look like his clothes had been through a shredding machine.

For the next following days, Bobby blocks out everything around him. He didn't eat much, he didn't talk to his friends, and he didn't even come out his room. He couldn't believe that his only brother was really gone. The only thing that he could do was cry. And that's just what he did. He cried day in and day out.

Bobby couldn't understand why his brother was shipped so abruptly. Anthony hadn't been in no trouble, none what so ever. To Bobby, something just didn't seem right; furthermore Anthony wasn't even finished with his court dates. So, how could they move him to another county and why?

The fact that his brother was gone and he knew he wouldn't see him for at least ten years or better. That really messed his mind up. He also knew this would be the last time the he would be able to hang out with his him. Things seemed to have turned from bad to worse for Bobby. Something wasn't right and he had to find out what was really going on.

Anthony was shipped to SMS JDC and this place was way worse than Freeman J.D.C. I mean these kids were bad. These kids was fighting each other and jumping on staff every day. SMS also had a very high turnover rate, nobody wanted to work at this place. Bobby heard the stories about this place and that only made him worry just that much more. All and all Bobby wasn't ready to let his only brother go yet.

Bobby wanted to talk to somebody about why his brother had to be shipped and he knew that Officer Coleman would be the most reliable and understanding person to turn to about this situation. After 3 or 4 days of not talking to nobody, he was ready to talk, so he went to Officer Coleman.

Bobby talked to Officer Coleman in the privacy of his room. There was no one else around. He thought Officer Coleman was very easy to talk to and was understanding of what he was going through. This of course put him at ease.

Bobby asked why his brother was shipped off. Officer Coleman looked at him and proceeded to explained to him that Anthony's life was in danger. Bobby looked confused, he didn't understand what Officer Coleman meant or what he was saying.

"I don't understand... in danger... in danger of what?"

Officer Coleman put his finger on his lips and said, "shhh."

He lowered his voice looked over his shoulder then turned back to Bobby, "well you know the little girl yo brother hit and killed?"

"Yeah, that was an accident. He didn't do that on purpose," Bobby says, interrupting.

Officer Coleman continued, "I know that it was an accident, but Tony is that little girl's cousin and the word on the concrete was Tony was planning on taking revenge out on your brother. It was so much talk about, that even administration heard about what Tony was planning to do... so admin had to do something to protect yo brother. So, Mr. Boykin had him shipped to another detention center. Bobby... it was for your brother's protection."

Bobby couldn't believe what he was hearing. He was even more infuriated than before. He remembered Tony had jumped on his brother and was making threats towards him, some weeks leading up to his brother being shipped. Anthony kept telling him to watch his back and not to trust no one. Then suddenly it all made since to him. But it still didn't make him feel no better.

CHAPTER 19

BOBBY'S NEW FRIEND

Several weeks after Anthony was shipped off, Bobby found out that his brother was sentenced to 15 years. Bobby was having a hard time dealing with all that was going on. For several days Bobby refused rec, leisure and food. He was in a deep depression. He felt like he got the 15 years.

The counselor of the facility tried to talk to him, but he would not open up to her. Bobby was totally in shut down mode. He wasn't talking to nobody. He was really hurt to the core.

Bobby's inability to communicate with anyone concerned the counselor, so as a precaution she thought it was a good idea to place Bobby on close observation. Close observation is a procedure that is put into place when an individual is a high risk candidate for self-harm also known as suicide. This is also referred to as a level one observation.

It is the responsibility of the assign officer to monitor the resident one on one, and document every 15-minute check. Ms. Jones (the counselor) didn't really believe that Bobby would hurt himself, but she wanted to be sure she covered all her basis.

For the next several days, Bobby was observed closely, consistent one on one. Over the next few days, he showed no signs of improvement. Nor did he show any signs of harming himself, so the counselor decided to clear him of close observation.

Ms. Jones tried very hard to figure out a way to get through to him and get him to open up to her. Every attempt she made didn't work. She tried all kinds of different techniques, but to no avail. Ms. Jones felt like she tried every trick in the book, but nothing seemed to work.

One day, while she was on her lunch break she had a light bulb moment- a good idea. There was a time when her friend, Mr. Wright came to the facility with his puppet named Sammy.

Mr. Wright did a group discussion with the boys and she remembered how much Bobby seemed to love this puppet.

Ms. Jones recalled Bobby telling Mr. Wright how much he liked the puppet and he was saying once he gets out the detention center, he was going to ask his mother to get him a doll just like Sammy.

I can ask Mr. Wright, if he would be willing to donate his puppet to the center for Bobby, she thought. She was confident under this situation; Mr. Wright would be more than willing to help.

So, Ms. Jones went right to work. Her first step was to get approval from administration and then the director. With no time to waste, Ms. Jones wrote Mr. Wright and explained the situation, as to why he was locked up in the first place. She also made it clear, that this boy was a straight A student who had never been in any trouble before.

Within three days of writing and submitting her letters, she had the approval from all parties, which she was very thankful. Ms. Jones then contacted Mr. Wright. After telling her plans to help Bobby, he told her that he would love to donate Sammy to Bobby. He remembered him and he made good on his word. Within two days, Ms. Jones had Sammy in her arms. She felt so good about doing all this for a young boy whom was in need of help. This is what she called an intervention in action. Doing all she could do to save a young life.

Today was the day, that Ms. Jones had been working so hard for. She was a little nervous because, she wasn't sure that her master plan would work. She wasn't sure how he would react to the doll, but she could only hope and pray for the best.

When she went to Bobby's room, he was doing the same thing that he had been doing since his brother left; absolutely nothing. Laying in his bed looking up at the ceiling. His room was filled with food and trash from days before. The counselor could tell that he hadn't been eating or taking showers; in addition to the food and trash in his room he looked very frail.

When she stepped inside his small cell she held the puppet behind her back, keeping it out of view. Bobby had no clue as to what Ms. Jones was up to.

"How are you doing today Bobby?"

"Um okay," he said, with his head down.

"Well- guess what Bobby? I have a special guest for you!"

"Um not in the mood to see anyone right now. Sorry."

She then showed him Sammy.

"Sammy!" Bobby said, in a loud cheerful voice.

He sat up in his bed reaching for the doll, with eyes wide and a big smile on his face that no one had seen in a long time.

"Thank you. Thank you- so much, Ms. Jones. I love him," he said, hugging his new puppet.

"Oh, you are so welcome Bobby. Mr. Wright donated him," said Ms. Jones with delight.

Bobby hugged and cuddled with his new friend with much enjoyment. Ms. Jones felt proud of the work she did to help him. To see him so happy was priceless to her.

The puppet was white with big brown eyes, black hair and rosy red lips and cheeks. It had on a black tuxedo suit. The doll was truly adorable. It stood 3 feet tall. Bobby sat there looking at the doll with all smile.

"Can I change has name Ms. Jones?" asked Bobby.

"Yeah sure, you can change his name to anything that you would like to. What name do you have in mind?"

He held and stared at the doll with joy. "I think-well, I think I want to call him Mr. Michael. Yeah, I like that... Mr. Michael!"

"Okay, very well, Mr. Michael is what it will be," she said, giving him a slap of the knee.

Bobby was so excited about having this puppet it was definitely therapy for him. After all he had been through, he was finally smiling again. Over the next day's Ms. Jones observed Bobby closely. She could see that he was making great progress, eating and talking again. He still choose to stay confined in his room but he was coming out to shower and that was a start.

The counselor saw this as a major step in the right direction. At the rate he was going, she knew that it was just a matter of time before he would be back to himself again.

Some weeks passed, then something happened; Bobby decided to come out his room to socialize with the other residents. Once the counselor saw him interacting with the others, she knew he was back to the old Bobby again. She also knew that she had made a smart decision to bring in Mr. Michael.

During the nights, it was easy for Bobby to go to his room for bed time. He looked forward to playing with his new friend; Mr. Michael. The doll made everything okay for him. It gave him a peace of mind.

CHAPTER 20

BOBBY'S GOING HOME

Early in the morning, while Bobby was washing his face and getting ready to start his day, a heavy knock on the door startled him. Bobby immediately rushed to the door to see who it was. The hall was quiet and there was no one at his door, or in the dayroom.

As he continued to stare out of his window he dried his face. He notices that there is a note on the floor of his room. Baffled, he paused for a moment. He looked out the window again. He saw no one. Then he picked up the note off the floor. He slowly unfolds the letter that someone had apparently slid under his door. His eyes pierced the lines of the letter which read in big red letters, "DON'T COME OUT YO ROOM- WE GONE BEAT YO FUCKING ASS."

Bobby's heart begin to race, he knew the only person behind this threat was Tony. His thoughts raced as he stares, at the bold red ink. In his mind, he felt that the red ink represented blood. He felt a chill go down his spin. This note made him very nervous. This wasn't just a note; no, this was a down outright threat.

Bobby knew that Tony was on a mission to get somebody back for killing his young cousin and since

he and his crew failed to get Anthony, they turned all their attention to Bobby. He just started coming out his room and things seem to have turn around for the better, now he has a hunt out on his head.

For Bobby, now the name of the game was just to survive until his release date, which was in a matter of three days. He decided to keep the note, so he could show it to Officer Coleman. He thought he should stay in his room and everything would be just fine. He figures they couldn't touch him as long as he stayed in his room.

Over the next several days, the staff brought everything that he needed to his room including soap, a change of clothes and food as well as snacks. There wasn't anything new going on in the dayroom, so he figured wasn't missing much at all. He really didn't feel like mixing and mingling anyway. He felt safe and secure in his own room. In his room he didn't have to worry about anybody trying to jump him or taking his food. He had Mr. Michael and that's all he needed.

He knew he wasn't coming out his room, until it was time for to take that walk to freedom. This was something that he had been waiting on for months and that's what kept him grounded. The fact that he

knew that it was almost over; soon he would a free man again.

On Sunday August 29, the sun was bright. It seemed brighter than ever outside of Bobby's window of his cell. He wakes up bright and early to a brand new day. This wasn't just any new day; no, this is a very special day. This is the day before his court date. So, what was so special about this day you might ask?

It wasn't because it was a hot summer day in August. It was the fact that Bobby was going to be released the following day, which of course would be Monday.

Yes, that's right he was finally getting out of this hell hole and going home to his loving mother. He had survived the concrete jungle. As he stared up at the clear blue sky on this quiet Sunday morning, he was taking it all in. His eyes shifted from the walls of his

5x7 cell and the beautiful blue sky to freedom. He thought about all that he had been through, all that he seen and all the things he had learned, which was a whole lot. He just felt so happy to be going home.

He thought about his brother and wondered what and how he was adjusting to the prison life. He

thought about his old friend Rudy. Every time he thought about Rudy it brought a smile to his face. That boy was crazy he thought to himself and of course at the same time it made him sad when he had the thoughts of the little girl that got hit and killed during that crazy high speed chase. But for the most part he survived and he became a stronger and better person through it all. A more spiritual person. This whole ordeal changed Bobby's life forever, and for the good.

This was the morning that Bobby said, "um free and um not running from nobody else."

He had made the decision that he didn't have to run, hide or stay cooped up in his room any more. Even though he had his mind made up about not running and hiding, he was still smart enough to keep Officer Coleman informed about the threat that was made against him in the letter. Officer Coleman assured Bobby that he would watch and keep an eye out for him. With this in mind, Bobby came out his room for the first time in days, since the threatening letter. He felt good knowing that he had a trusted officer watching his back. Over all, he was just excited because he was getting out and going home the next

day and he wasn't about to let no one steal his joy away.

That morning Bobby went to church. "How is everyone doing," said the preacher to the group of boys. Some of the boys in the group were still coming into the dining area as the preacher begins to speak. The preacher is a well-dressed man in a black suit, he looks to be between the age of 30- 35.

He was also accompanied by another young man, but this man was dressed casual and looks a lot younger than the preacher. The preacher starts off by asking the group to stand up for prayer and then he asks, "how many of you all know that God is good and that he has a plan for your life?"

"All the time God is good," said the other man with the preacher.

"My name is Dr. Williams. I want to start off by telling you all a little about myself. When I was young, just about your age. I was in and out of places like this. In fact, I was in this same very place and I wasn't a preacher back then."

The group giggles. "It wasn't until I almost went to prison when I decided to take things serious. I

changed my ways. I changed my way of thinking. I change my friends and I changed my life. It's time for you, young men to do the same."

The boys appeared to be surprised when he said, that he was in the same place. The preacher went on to say, "how many of you all know that God is still good?"

Some of the group responded by rising their hands and the others mumbled in agreement.

"He's not good just when things are going good in your life, God is good all the time. God is good even when your world seem to be turning upside down, but God can turn your world right side up. God is always good," the preacher repeated.

The preacher then pulled out his bible and turned a few pages. "I want to talk to you all about the company you keep. How many of you all know you should keep good company? The company you keep can something determine how far you go in life. So, understand how important it is to keep good company."

He pauses for a moment, then he tells the boys to open their bibles to a verse. The boys follow the

man's instructions. The preacher waited patiently for the boys to find the bible verse as he begins to read the verse. Once he's done, he looks up.

"Birds of a feather flock together. Do you know what that mean?" he asked, the group of boys.

The preacher asked the boys to repeat after him, "Birds of a feather flock together."

The boys participate saying, "birds of a feather flock together," the boys repeated in unison.

"I'll say it again, birds of a feather flock together. It doesn't say the bad hang out with the good, nor does it say the weak hang out with the strong. Again it says, birds of a feather flock together."

The dining area was very quiet, so much that one could hear a pin drop. The boys appear to be captivated by the preacher.

"So, that means in my mind, if you ain't no crack head, why would you be running around with crack heads?" The room is filled with laughter.

"If you running around with crack heads, it won't be long before you become a crack head." The laughter continues.

"That's just the way that works. Y'all think it's funny but um being real. If you not a drug dealer or a drug user, you ain't got no business running with one. This rule goes the same for being successful. If you want to be successful, you have to get to know some successful people. You don't ever see winners running with losers. It's like oil and water. What happens when you try to mix oil and water?" The preacher asked the group.

The residents sit quietly, looking at one another. "Come on!" he announced, "I know somebody can tell me the answer."

Then one boy raised his hand. He points to the boy. "Water and oil don't mix, it separates."

"Exactly! - I couldn't have said it any better. How many of you all know some of y'all need to separate? Um talking about separation. Y'all, um talking about separating from your negative thinking, negative behavior. Um talking about separating from your self-pity. Um talking about separating from yo self-destruction ways. Separate means to discontinue, to get away from, it means giving it up- for good. Letting go. Um talking about change in all of your lives. Yes, change- change for the better." The preacher paused

then wiped his mouth with a handkerchief he pulled out his jacket.

"Some of y'all need to separate from your friends. Sometimes you need to separate from your family. Now y'all looking at me like um crazy."

"I know that's right preacher," an officer says, putting his two cents in.

"Don't look at me like um crazy, I ain't doing nothing but telling the truth. See, some of y'all are scared of the truth. Let me tell y'all a little something. The truth ain't gone hurt nobody. Y'all running around here doing any and everything trying to impress your friends. Your trying to get your rep up and them same friends you trying to impress, talking bout you like a dog behind your back. Probably trying to get yo girl-friend while you locked up."

  Some of the boys smile, while the others seemed like to not like that statement. "Them so called friends y'all trying to impress, is running to the police telling them all about you. Lying on you and everything else. Trying to jump on yo case so they can get they're time cut short." The boys found that to be on point, because they know the preacher was telling the truth.

  "Y'all laughing because some of y'all know um telling the truth and some of y'all might be the very one's around here snitching."

  The dining room is filled with another outburst of laughter. The man looks at everyone in the room, including the officer. "Come on. Y'all don't get all quiet on me now. I aint doing nothing, but telling the truth. I ain't going to take up too much of you all time."

"Take yo time and preach, these bad jokers ain't got anything else to do today," an officer yells out from the back of the room.

"I know y'all got games and BET y'all want to watch, so I aint gone be too much longer. It wasn't until I almost went to prison before I realized I had to do a separation from a whole lot of things. I almost had to do a separation from myself. Every time I went to juvenile, none of my friends came to visit me. They didn't even take the time to write me a letter to see how I was doing. But every time I got out of jail, the first thing they wanted me to do was get high and run the streets. The next thing I knew, I was right back locked up again. So, I had to come to the conclusion: I had to make a change. I had to separate from my homeboys, because I was heading straight to prison. The only thing my friends wanted to do was rob, steal and mob, and because I was the youngest they would put everything off on me. Like a dummy, I did it. I did everything and anything they told me to. I was so busy trying to be cool and impress a bunch of guys who didn't care nothing about me. I went alone with anything they said. If they would have told me to rob my own mama, I probably would have done it. That's how bad it was. I got tired of being a foolish follower, so one day in jail, the man says in a slower calming tone, "I decided to be a leader when I get out of jail. As soon as I touched down; here they come, my so called boys, talking about sum man let's get high. Let's pop this. Let's pop that. I wanted to pop those suckers upside the head," he says with a smile.

"I finally realized all they wanted to do was get me in a whole lot of trouble. They wasn't ever talking about nothing positive. It was all negative thinking, which lead to negative action."

The man stood there looking at the group. "I made up my mind to be like oil and I separated from the water. Yeah, they talked about me like a dog, but I didn't care. I just kept it moving and guess what? I finished school and I ain't been back to jail since. You can do the same thing. It wasn't easy, but going back and forth to jail isn't easy either. You got to have God on your side to guide you and strengthen you. Young men, always remember this, you have two kinds of people in the world. You have the people that chase their dreams and you have people that kill the dreams. Which one are you? Ain't God good? I'll tell you again, you gots to have God on your side to guide you and strengthen you. I realized that those dudes weren't my friends at all. I realized they was all bad company. You see, a lot of y'all have bad company in your life. Right now, you got bad company up in your life! But, um here to tell you, the only company you really need is God's company," he says louder.

"Ain't God good? Ain't God good?" he repeated.

"Amen," the group says in agreement with the preacher. Then the preacher holds up his bible in his right hand and says, "let us pray now- please bow your heads. Stand up for God. If you don't stand up something you will fall for anything," he adds, as the boys slowly stand to their feet. The preacher begins to pray for the group, then church was dismissed. After church was over the group went back to the unit and did what they always do after church. They cleaned their rooms and the unit. This day Bobby thought it was strange that Tony and his crew wasn't harassing him or paying him any attention. Just some days ago one of them sled a note under his door saying, that they was going to get him. Then he thought, that maybe it wasn't Tony or it was just a stupid prank. He wasn't too much worried about them, because he knew that Officer Coleman had his back and he wasn't going to let nothing happen to him.

While Bobby was at leisure time, Officer Coleman called out to him. Bobby was sitting at the table talking to his friend.

"Bobby!" Officer Coleman called out.

"What's up Officer Coleman?"

"Listen, I just got a phone call from the house. I have to leave right now. Do you want to go to your room for the rest of the evening?"

Bobby looked at Officer Coleman, then looked around the dayroom, everything looked to be cool and he felt there was no reason to be worried about anything. He looked back at Officer Coleman and told him, "No, I think I'll be fine."

"Are you sure Bobby? Because I can put you in your room before I go."

"Nall, um good. Thank you," Bobby answered.

Officer Coleman then looked over at Officer Simms and told him he was about to dip and told him to keep an out eye for Bobby and of course, he did agree to do so. Just before Officer Coleman exited the door, he turned and said to Bobby with a big smile on his face, "oh yeah you going home tomorrow, make sure you stay in touch with us now and good luck. Do good out there."

"Yes sir," he said with the biggest smile ever. "I will," he added.

Bobby felt okay to stay out because all day Tony was no longer trying to bother him. He felt that, if he wanted to do something to him he could have done it already. He had all the opportunity to do something, he thought. So, from that he wasn't worried about nothing. Besides, today was Sunday. A great day and tomorrow would be Monday, an even better day. He would be free again, so he was happy and he wasn't going to let nothing mess up his day.

Later that night, during shower time, Bobby begins to feel strange. He begins to feel as though something wasn't right. For whatever reason, he just didn't feel right about taking a shower that night. It was something deep inside him saying don't get in that shower tonight. Just go to your room. He figured maybe just maybe, he was anxious about getting out of jail tomorrow or maybe it was because, that evil

Officer Johnson was running showers that night. Officer Johnson held this crazy deranged look in his eyes, topped off with this nasty smirk on his face, while sitting there staring directly at Bobby. It was the look that would make anybody nervous. He decides to just ignore that inter voice and went on about his business.

"Last call for showers. If you want to take a shower come on!" Officer Johnson called to the dayroom where most of the group of boys had already showered.

"I need one more for the shower!" he added.

Bobby slowly gets up with his hands full of hygiene items and makes his way towards the shower. His plan was to take a quick shower. In and out, get his snacks and go to bed early, because he knows he has a big day tomorrow.

Bobby grabs his hygiene items and a set of fresh clothes. He then goes into the shower. As he entered he noticed that Eddy was the only one in the shower laughing and singing cheerfully. Bobby speaks to him, but he seemed not to notice him, because he was busy washing his hair, singing and having a good ole time.

As he begins to undress and start taking his shower, he saw Marcus come into the shower. Moments later, Larry and Patrick entered. Bobby begins to feel very uneasy about his decision to shower at this point. Suddenly Officer Johnson appears looking at him directly in his eyes with that evil smile. He gives him a nod, as to say I told you I was going to get yo ass back.

Shaking and scared Bobby looks back at Officer Johnson with tears in his eyes. Officer Johnson suddenly leaves the area. As he did, Tony walked into the shower fully dressed. By now, Eddy is just looking with his eyes full of fear, even he can sense that something bad was about to happen.

"Yeah, yo bitch ass brother got out, but you bout to get it. Bitch ass nigga," Tony says, walking towards him with his fist balled up. He was smacking his fist into the palm of his left hand.

Bobby attempted to make a run for it, as he tries to pass the threating boys, he slips on the wet floor almost falling.

"Get that pussy ass nigga!" Tony tells his crew, shutting the door behind him.

Eddy looks in terror, yelling for help as the drama begins to unfold.

Marcus walks over to him with the water still running and tells Eddy, "shut the fuck up!" he said in a threating matter.

With his back against the wall. Eddy slid down and put his head between his knees, as to take cover.

"You know this lame as nigga gone run and tells," Larry says to Tony.

"Man- fuck that nigga, ain't nobody gone believe his retarded ass."

"That nigga scared anyway. He ain't gone say shit," Marcus added.

Tony and his boys have Bobby cornered with no staff present. The only other person that is present is Eddy. Apparently, this was all a part of Officer Johnson and Tony's evil plan.

As Bobby try to exit the shower, the boys commence to beating Bobby down. The boys begin kicking and hitting him; targeting his head and upper body. As the boys unleased a flurry of violate blows, Bobby yells to the top of voice for help.

"Help! Help! - Somebody please help me!" badly beaten, he cries out as the vicious blows come from every direction.

The sound of the boy's blows echo throughout the shower like a drummer beating a drum. Eddy watches the brutal beating helplessly. With every other blow, Bobby's blood is splattered against the shower walls and runs down the shower drain. This is quickly becoming a bloody scene.

As Bobby knees begin to buckle, Tony throw a right fist that connect with the left side of Bobby's face disconnecting his jaw bone. Two teeth fly out of his mouth hitting the wall, dropping him instantly. Just as he falls to the floor, Officer Johnson peeks in witnessing the brutal attack. He does nothing to try to stop the assault, in fact he stands to the side of the hall to make sure no one comes to the shower area.

As Bobby falls to the floor, the group of boys begins to kick and stomp him, as if they were playing a game of street soccer. At this point, Bobby is totally defenseless. He's begging and pleading for his life.

While the assault is taking place, Officer Johnson goes into an empty room next to the shower and begins to talk on his cell phone, which he wasn't supposed to be using or have in the facility.

Eddy's eyes are filled with horror, as he witnessed the assault unfold. He tries to yell for help, but terror chokes his throat. No matter how hard he tries to scream, no sound can escape his mouth. He can't scream, nor can he move. He is paralyzed by fear.

The beating continued for several more minutes, but seemed like eternity. After several severe blows to the head, neck and body, Bobby laid there in a big puddle of blood motionless. His blood flowed out of his head like a flowing river. He was shaking and

gasping for air, trying to hold on for dear life. Both of his eyes swollen shut. His body badly beaten. Unclothed and beaten, his life is becoming breathless.

Marcus and Patrick quickly run out the shower, looking back at Bobby. With blood all over them, they run into the next room where Officer Johnson was already waiting still talking on the phone. They begin to laugh and tell Officer Johnson about the brutal attack, as they clean up, washing the blood and evidence away.

"Boy! We beat that nigga ass."

Back in the shower the walls are covered with blood. Bobby isn't moving. His body seemed to be lifeless.

"Let go bruh-this nigga bout dead shawty," Larry says, to Tony breathing deeply, bent over with his hands on his knees. He's trying to catch his breath with blood and sweat dripping from his face.

"Grab his legs!" Tony demanded.

"What the fuck you doing bruh?" Larry asked.

"Man just grab his fuckin legs bruh!"

Now Tony, Larry and Eddy are the only ones that are in the shower with the beaten victim. Larry is trying to get Tony out of the shower before someone catches them; however Tony refuses to leave the area. Tony then grabs Bobby under the arms and begins to drag him, as if he was going to pull him out of the shower. As Tony move, Bobby, he moans and mummers sounds. It's obvious he is in excruciating pain, and has been beaten to a state of unconsciousness. As Tony gets to the threshold of the door, he stopped. All the while, Eddy and Larry are breathing frantically, waiting to see what Tony was going to do next.

"Fuck you doing shawty? Let's get the fuck out of here!" Larry pleaded with Tony again.

Tony looks up at him, but there is no response. Only an evil soulless look in his eyes. Suddenly Tony grabs the twenty-pound steel metal door with both hands, looks down at Bobby's bloody frame and says, "this is for my lil cousin fuck boy."

Then with all he had, he slammed the door on Bobby's head crushing his skull like an egg shell. The force from the impact kills him instantly. Blood and brain matter splatters all over the boys and the walls.

Larry is in total disbelief to what he just witnessed. A murder. A murder that was not supposed to happened. But now, he was involved. In the back ground Eddy is going crazy, yelling, screaming and going hysterical.

"Tony! What the fuck is wrong with you? Why the fuck you kill him?" Larry asked.

Tony looked straight into Larry eyes with blood dripping from his face and said and a whisper like tone, "I didn't kill him, we killed him."

Chills went down Larry's spine. Now he realized that he have crossed the point of no return. The two boys then dragged Bobby back into the shower. Then Tony told Larry to wash the blood off himself, as he did the same. Both boys gain their composer, as if nothing ever happened. Eddy sat in shock and was speechless.

Tony and Larry took their time cleaning up the bloody mess, in the shower. After cleaning up, the two boys staged it to look like an accident. The two boys then ran out the shower into the dayroom, in a make believe panic. They started yelling for help saying, "Bobby had an accident. Bobby had an accident in the shower!" they both yelled.

The officers including Officer Johnson ran into the shower to investigate the boys claim. Upon the officers' arrival, they all witnessed a very violent crime scene. Bobby's lifeless bloody body laid there, in a pool of blood. Blood and brain matter was all over him. Eddy was still sitting there in shock, motionless and speechless. He was still shaking.

The facility went on emergency lock down immediately. Pictures of the crime scene were taken and the investigation was on. The facility was to be locked down until the investigation was completed.

When the officer asked the four residents what happened, the boys all shared the same story; which was they all claim that Bobby and Eddy was horse playing and the shower, then the two boys start fighting. Then Bobby slipped on some shampoo on the floor busting his head. All the boys said the same thing including Officer Johnson. They also wrote incident statements, stating the same story. When the investigating officers asked Eddy what happened, he didn't say a single word. He was so shaken up that he couldn't even speak. He was still in shock. He was later sent to medical for observation. For the next days to come Eddy, would not come out of his room.

He was afraid that the boys were going to get him next. He didn't talk to nobody.

All the necessary reports and paper work was filled out and filed. The police and the Georgia Bureau of Investigation were called to the scene.

CHAPTER 21

THE BIG COVER UP

It was not long, before Officer Johnson found out that there was a plot to seek revenge on Bobby that got out of hand and it went too far. Tony, the ring leader took things into his own hands. Officer Johnson and the other boys thought that this would be just a good ole fashion butt whooping. But Tony on the other hand, had his own ulterior motive. He told them that killing Bobby was part of his game plan from the beginning, only because they had shipped Anthony away, before they could get him. Tony also expressed he knew that the younger brother was innocent, but he didn't give a fuck. He wanted to get him before he got out of jail and that's exactly what he did.

So, it turns out that the four juveniles and an officer have an investigation going on against them for a possible murder case. Officer Johnson knows if the facts and the truth come out to light, he could spend the rest of his natural life locked up behind bars. Just the thought of this made him sick to his stomach. He and the boys devise a plan to cover up the truth, so nobody would have to do any time. Not only was Officer Johnson facing possible prison time, but also he had to face Mr. Boykin which was really the least of his problems.

"Johnson- man what the fuck did you do this time?" Mr. Boykin screams at the top of his voice as Officer Johnson walks into his office the following morning.

"I swear- Mr. B it was an accident," Officer Johnson replied.

"An accident! Bumping into someone is an accident. That wasn't a damn accident. You done let somebody get murdered in this damn place. Shut my door."

Officer Johnson walk's into Mr. Boykin office, knowing that he is about to get his butt chewed up and spit out.

"They... they was just pose to ruff the boy up a little-man. They took the shit too far. That was not supposed to happen," said Officer Johnson, lowering his head in shame. "I didn't know they was going to fucking kill him. That wasn't part of the plan. I swear Mr. B."

Officer Johnson was indeed a crooked officer, but even he wasn't that low to intentionally let somebody get killed.

"You let them damn kids fight in the shower?" Mr. Boykin asked, "I don't give a shit, what they do back there. I don't give a damn. You done got yo dumb ass caught up in some shit. I had to call this boy's mother and tell her, her damn son done got killed in this damn place!" Mr. Boykin was beyond angry. "Don't you know you can go to the pen for this bullshit?" he added.

Mr. Boykin is fired up at this point. "I got the good mind to fire yo monkey ass right now," he says, wiping sweat from his forehead.

"We can work this out Mr. B."

"We can work this out! This ain't no fucking we. We ain't got shit to do with this!" Mr. Boykin said, abruptly interrupting Officer Johnson.

Mr. Boykin is trying with all his might not to jump on the officer. He is just that pissed off. He takes a deep breath, as he takes a moment to compose himself.

"I guess the counselors had heard his brother was in trouble, that Tony was planning on jumping him, cause Anthony killed his cousin. They had him shipped. And they killed Bobby because they couldn't get to Anthony," he says, as if was thinking out loud, trying to make sense out of this crazy situation. "They wasn't pose to kill him. It was just supposed to be a beat down and that's it. That's the whole truth... man you got to help me out on this one. Me and you done a lot of illegal shit up in here together. Man you got to help me out," Officer Johnson pleaded.

"When all this was going on, where the hell was you?" asked Mr. Boykin.

"I was doing showers when it happened. I didn't see it," he replied.

"Do you know how the fuck you sound right now? Yo ass is dumber than I thought. How the hell you didn't see it?" asked Mr. Boykin

"I was in an empty cell using my cell phone. When I came back to the shower area blood and shit was everywhere," he said, trying to sound convincing.

Mr. Boykin became more upset by the minute. "Damn, you a big fuck up!"

Mr. Boykin proceeded to ask more questions, "who all was in the shower?"

"Nobody but Tony, Larry, Marcus, Patrick and that retarded kid Eddy."

"Who?" Mr. Boykin replied.

"Eddy. You know the crazy one."

"Oh yeah, I know who he is. His crazy ass. Are you sure that nobody else was there or no one else seen anything?"

"Yeah, um sure, nobody knows what went down. The dayroom was already locked down on this night," says, the crooked officer.

"You sure?" Mr. Boykin asked again.

"Yes, we cleaned everything up. It looked like they was in there playing around. You know, there's no camera in that area," the officer said, feeling a little more confident, as he explained.

"Yeah- I know," Mr. Boykin replied, rubbing his chin.

"Look Mr. B, if you can just harry up and ship Eddy we'll be good. Look, he already scared and he ain't talking to nobody. I wrote a witness statement and made him sign it. You know that boy can't read or write a lick," Officer Johnson said, feeling more and more confident Mr. Boykin maybe on his side.

"Okay, okay," Mr. Boykin says, putting both his hands up, cutting the officer off.

"We may can slip through the cracks on this one. I'll make some phones calls in the morning and see what happens."

"Once he is gone, I think we will be good. Besides, I don't think that GBI would take his word anyway. Especially since he already signed that statement," Officer Johnson added.

"Yeah, you may be right Johnson, but I can't afford to take any chances," Mr. Boykin added.

"Where you gone send him too?" Officer Johnson asked.

"It doesn't matter. To somebody's crazy house down the road," Mr. Boykin replied. Looking out his office window, as if he was in deep thought, Mr. Boykin leaned into Officer Johnson to tell him in a low voice, "the next time you get in some bullshit, yo ass is gone. You be on yo own," he looks at him and says, "I promise you that- frat brother or not."

"Yes sir. Yes sir. Thank you for having my back my brother," Officer Johnson says and then sighs in relief.

Mr. Boykin walks over to the door of his office and opens it up and tells Officer Johnson, "now get the fuck out my office!"

The officer says nothing in return. Just as Mr. Boykin promised, in matter of days Eddy was shipped off and was never heard from again.

CHAPTER 22

THE INVESTIGATION

Within a matter of days of the suspicious death of resident Bobby Berry, GBI (Georgia Bureau of Investigation) had set off a full-fledged investigation on the death of one of its own residents. Freeman JDC was crawling with GBI agents, not to mention the news media had a field day. They were set up just outside the fence. The facility was on locked down, no juveniles where coming out of their rooms with the exception of the ones who had court dates.

Every person in the building was interviewed and integrated and I mean everybody from the residents to the staff. GBI was there every day looking for clues that would lead to the truth. When the investigators got to Officer Johnson, Tony and his boys - they already had information: what, when, where and why all together. Officer Johnson had prep the boys on everything they needed to know and say. He ensured the boys that Mr. Boykin had their backs, so the boys felt strong that they would get off without any additional charges.

The interview:

Please state your full name and tell me, what did you see?" asked Detective Davis, staring down on Tony sipping on a cup of Joe. Mr. Davis had been a detective for more than twenty years.

"My name is Tony Wright. It was me, Larry, Marcus, Patrick, Bobby and Eddy," Tony replied rocking back and forth in a nervous state.

"Where was Officer Johnson?"

"He was right there," he says, as his eyes shifted from the floor back to the detective, trying his best to avoid direct eye contact.

"You seemed to be pretty damn nervous son," Mr. Davis says, getting eye level with the kid. "Tell me what happened in the shower on Sunday 29 of August- and I only want to know the truth," he added.

"I'm gone tell you the truth sir," he then takes a deep breath, as if it was his last breath. "It was me and the others boys. "

"What other boys- be specific!" the other detective called in a roar, which was Detective Butler. Mr. Butler was relevantly new to the force. He had been with the GBI for only five years.

"The same ones, I already that I already told you. It was me, Larry, Patrick, Bobby, Marcus and Eddy. We was all taking our showers and Bobby and Eddy started playing in the shower. They was play fighting at first, then they start fighting for real. Bobby hit Eddy and then he tried to run."

"Who tried to run and where do you supposed he was trying to run to?" Detective Davis asked. Peering right into Tony's shifting eyes.

"Bobby was trying to run and get out of the shower," Tony replied. Minute by minute, sweat rings begins to appear under Tony's arm pits, as sweat beads pop from his forehead. At this point, Tony is defiantly nervous. The two detectives exchange looks, as to say we both know this kid isn't being honest.

"Officer Johnson was sitting in a chair, like in the door way."

"Was he there the whole time? Was Officer Johnson in the shower with you all?" Detective Davis asked.

"No, he was outside the door, but he could see inside the shower. He seen the whole thing- I swear," he pleaded holding up his left hand.

"So, how did Bobby get all those bruises all over his body? Please explain that," asked Detective Butler.

"I don't know," Tony said, dropping his head, trying to look convincing. Tony knew he had to put on the act of his life, because he was facing the possibility of life in prison. "They were fighting. Bobby and Eddy. People get bruises when they are fighting," he said it with a serious look on his face, as he looked in Detective Butler in the eyes.

"You was in there. How you don't know what happened?" Detective Butler screams, interrupting the boy in questioning standing to his feet.

"I told you Bobby and Eddy was play fighting."

"You don't get those kind of bruises from playing. They was doing more than playing around. Somebody beat the living shit out that kid," Detective Davis said, whipping sweat away from his forehand with the hill of his right palm.

"We think you are lying through your teeth," Detective Davis roared again, seeming to become more agitated by the minute.

"Um not lying to you. Just look at the cameras," tears begin to stream from Tony's lying eyes. "Um telling you the truth and that's all I know. I didn't have shit to do with nobody dying," Tony said, laying his head in his folded arms on the table.

"You're lying. You killed Bobby because his brother killed your cousin on accident! And that was an accident. You and your fucking boys killed Bobby and you know it!" Detective Davis exploded.

"We gone get to the bottom of this and when we do, we gone prosecute everyone that was involved in this murder including that dirty ass Johnson!" The detective says, in a raging tone.

Tony begins to sob uncontrollable. He has broken all the way down.

"Take this lying piece of shit back to the unit," Mr. Davis yells to the officer, standing outside of the interview room, which was Officer Simms.

Both the detectives have a strong feeling that this was no accident. Not an accident at all. It was with no doubt in the detectives' minds, a vicious murder. Murder one. Both the men know that a hunch wouldn't stand in the court of law. This was something that would have to be proven and they had every intention of proving that this was a murder beyond a reasonable doubt.

What they needed was a confession. A confession from Officer Johnson or at least one of the boys. So, the detectives plan was to identify the weakest link of the group and play a friendly game of divide and concur. The investigators knew the only chance of getting down to the truth of what really happened, was to get the officer and the boys to turn on one another and offer the first one a deal.

After interviewing Tony, the ring leader of the crew, the GBI interviewed Marcus and Larry next. Patrick was the last to be interviewed, and of course his story was no different from the other boys. All the boy's shared very similar stores to Tony's. The detectives tried every method they could think of to get the boys to tell the truth. Even offering less time for the person that would participate with the GBI. Much to the detective's surprise this would be a tougher case to solve than they anticipated. These residents weren't talking at all. The threats, the offers, it didn't matter. These boys' lips were sealed and that was that.

Officer Johnson was the last of the group to be interviewed. But just as the boys' stated, Officer Johnson gave the same story. He wasn't telling anything. Nothing but lies and a well put together story.

Officer Johnson stated that while he was conducting showers, Bobby and Eddy begin to horse play. "I gave them both several directives to stop horse playing, but they just kept playing until something bad happened," he said.

He then told the investigators, "at first the two boys looked to be just playing around, then Bobby hit Eddy pretty hard then the two begin to fight for real. Bobby tried to run that's when he slipped on some shampoo, fell and busted his head."

Officer Johnson also claimed that Bobby was his favorite resident. When the investigators brought up the fact that Bobby had wrote a grievance on him and got him suspended, he stated that they both had long made up after that. He and the boy was cool with each other. The detectives tried to rattle Officer Johnson, but he was unmoved. He gave them absolutely nothing.

The GBI detectives didn't know that these guys had everything laid out. Mr. Boykin had coached them on all they needed to say and what not to say. He also drilled them in telling them without proof the GBI would have to prove their case beyond the shadow of any doubt in the court of law. Since the group knew that the cameras weren't working in that area, they knew they had a great chance of getting away with murder.

The conclusion:

After weeks and weeks of questioning and interviewing everyone and turning over every stone, the GBI investigators came with their findings or lack of. When it was all said and done, the case was thrown out due to a lack of evidence. The case was declared closed. It was determined that Bobby's death was an accident. The official ruling was accidental death. Holding no one responsible. Exonerating all parties involved with the case. When Bobby's mother heard the news, she was very hurt and it was if she was living through a nightmare. She did the only thing she knew to do and that was to take legal action against the officer and the county in a wrongful death law suit. Tony planned and executed the perfect murder and they all got away with it.

After the conclusion of the investigation, the facility lock down was lifted and things where back on a regular schedule again. Officer Coleman had a very difficult time dealing with Bobby's death. He blamed himself, because he felt that he was the one person that should have been looking out for Bobby. He tried his hardest to move pass the death, but he just couldn't do it. As a result, two weeks after the investigation was over, he left the center never to be heard from again.

The residents were so happy to be coming out their rooms, they didn't know what to do. They were just happy to go outside for rec, play games and watch TV. For a long time, none of the residents wanted to use that room that Bobby had nor did nobody want to go into the shower.

Bobby's room was cleaned out and made for use again. His personal belongings were packed and sent to his mother. But one thing really strange happened, when Bobby died, the staff immediately locked down the whole facility including Bobby's room, which was room C-zero six (C-06). When the staff cleaned and bagged all his property, no one could find his three foot ventriloquist doll: Mr. Michael. The staff spent hours looking for this doll, yet it was nowhere to be found. They questioned all the residents. They all said the same thing, the last time the doll was seen was in Bobby's room. But yet, the doll was missing. Did someone steal it? Did someone hide it? Those were the big questions. All everybody knew was, it was missing. Mr. Michael was never found.

CHAPTER 23

3 MONTHS LATER

By early October, the leaves are falling from the trees and the wind begins blow. The weather was changing and winter is peaking in. It's beginning to become very cold outside. The kind of cold that freeze you to the core of your bones. Even a coat is defenseless in this kind of weather. The mood of the unit has also shifted. Everything seemed to be a lot more laid back. It's funny, how the weather outside effect the residents mood on the inside.

Some days later, the snow begins to fall. The snow is a big deal in the south. In Atlanta, it never snows in this part of the south. So, when there is any kind of sign of snow, they prepare to shut the city down. I mean all the way down. Schools are dismissed early. State and city officials close early. When the snow begins to fall it is a state of emergency. Everything is closed down. Businesses, Wal-Mart, gas stations even the clubs shut down. And that's with only two inches on the ground.

"Y'all look! It's snowing outside!" Officer Simms says, peering through the window in the dayroom.

"Wow! It's coming down fo show," Officer Parker replied, "I just hope that the snow don't stick."

As Officer Parker walked over to the window, he could see the snow falling for himself. Excited! He turned around to everyone and announced that it was snowing outside. The group of boys rushed to the window to get a glimpse of the snow. For some the boys, this the first time they ever seen any snow in person and for others snow wasn't a big deal at all. For the residents who appreciated the winter bliss they stared at the snow with joy and smiles on their young faces.

"Ooh, can we go outside tomorrow?" the group of boys pleaded cheerfully.

"Um not sure just how cold it will be tomorrow. We will have to see," an officer replied, "I also have to see how y'all act."

"Yeah, that would be fun to go outside to run and play in the snow. We could even have a snow fight," one boy says with eyes focus on the falling snow.

"Man- shut yo five- year- old ass up nigga," a voice calls out from the dayroom. Laughter follows. "This nigga sound like a damn kindergartener."

The group shares a laugh at the expense of the other boy.

As the hours drags on, the snow becomes thicker and heavier.   By this time, the sky was filled with snowflakes. The officers rushed to the control room to listen to the weather radio.   According to the weather forecast, there are no signs of the snowy condition slowing down anytime soon.

The following day, the officers decided to allow the residents some free time outside for rec.   The residents had been cooped up inside the unit for several days and they all had a bad case of cabin fever. The boys were so excited to be going out and no one refused to go outside.   At this time, the snow had fallen about one foot deep and it was still falling. The cold was brutal and the wind whipped right through the residents thin coats. The boys didn't care about the cold, they were too busy having fun, running, playing and having snowball fights like young children. Even Tony and his crew could not resist the urge to play in winter's joy.

You wouldn't have thought that most of these teens are hardcore criminals, by the way they danced, laughed and played in the pure white fluffy snow. It was as though their slates had been wiped clean. In that moment, the juveniles ran and played with such innocence and joy, like they had not a care in the world. I guess for the moment they were free. Yes free indeed, free as you or me. Free as a bird carried by the warm summer breeze beneath its wings. Some of the kids caught snowflakes in their hands, while others looked up at the heavens with their mouths wide open as to hope of catching snowflakes. It is true that it was freezing cold outside, but the joy of winter warmed their hearts. As the kids played and danced you can see the reminiscence of innocence the children somehow lost and got corrupted somewhere along the way in their young lives.

The sound of a whistle fills the winter skies. "Line up!" Officer Johnson yelled, as a puff of cloud like smoke floats out his mouth into the depth of the cold. "It's time to take it in," he added, with his teeth chattering from the cold rubbing his hands together.

"Can we stay out for a little longer," a couple of the boys requested, as they begin to form a line along the gated fence.

"Hell nall. It's colder than a muthafucka out here. It's time to take that shit in," Officer Hill announced.

The officers on the rec yard begin to call off the unit halls to bring the boys inside the building. "B, C, D line it up," an officer called out.

"Let's get right," one boy shouts, rubbing his hands, trying to generate heat in this bone chilling weather.

"It's cold as hell out here- shawty," another boy added.

"Y'all better line y'all asses, before y'all asses get left out here," Officer Simms announces. The residents begin to settle down and fall in line, at the command of the officer's voice. The residents slowly move into the building. While moving into the building some of the residents look back at the snow, which was still falling. Suddenly the mood of the environment turns to somber. Reality begins to set in again.

Some resident's moaned while others complained. It was clear to see that no one wanted to be on that stinky unit. The young males would have preferred to be standing outside in the cold, than to be on the unit.

The following day, the officers all gathered around the dining table to discuss the real possibility of a full fledge winter storm. This was something that the city of Atlanta isn't equip for. The officers watched the weather channel for the latest developments. According to the weather report, this would be the worst storm that Georgia has ever seen.

As the officer's watched the weather report, it said that the storm was coming in from the mid-west. The worst of it would be coming in the next two to three days. At once, the officers begin to prepare for the big winter blast. The officers begin to check the backup generators. The central control officer listens closely to the weather radio for any developing stories. One officer was sent to the armor room to get extra flood lights and flash lights. The kitchen pantries were already stocked with nonperishable foods and water. The others retrieved extra sheets and blankets. Now, the group of officers are ready for the worst that could happen.

Three days later, much to the group surprise, the weather man was right, just as he predicted, it snowed, snowed and snowed some more. Everyone was caught off guard by the mass of snow that fell. Even though they all got ready for the storm, no one was really ready or prepared for the crazy things that was about to unfold. All the officers knew; this was no time to be fighting or fussing amongst each other.

They all banded together, so they could survive though this snow storm. Everyone was ready to contribute and work as a team.

During this time the staff was well prepared for the snow. They had all the emergency equipment ready, completed with fully charged flashlights, flood lights, down to the backup batteries. Needless to say, the staff of Freeman JDC was ready for whatever.

The residents didn't seem to mind the storm. All it meant for them was more leisure time. During this time, the last thing the staff needed was a bunch of hard head bad juveniles running up and down the halls and fighting. So, the officers did any and everything they could to keep the juveniles calm and quiet. The residents watched a lot of TV and played even more PlayStation and inside board games.

One day during leisure time, the dayroom was dim and was filled with the residents watching a movie. The officers were in the dayroom with the boys as usual.

As the boys sat quietly watching the movie, one boy begins to say, "the evil is near us," in a whisper and in a very low but dragging tone. The boys sitting next to him did not react. They continued watching the movie. Seconds later, the boy whispered again, "the force of evil is close at hand." The resident sitting on the boy's right side placed his finger to his mouth, as to say, shhhh. "The evil is coming," he whispered again, with a look in his eyes, as if his soul was separated from his body.

 "What? Man be quiet," the boy replied sitting beside him.

"He's here," he whispered again, but this time in a much deeper voice almost in a demoniac like voice. By this time, the other boys are raising their hands trying to get the officer's attention.

 Officer Simms looked over and ask, "what do y'all need?"

"Um trying to watch the movie, but this dude keeps on talking."

"Hey man, if you want to watch this movie you gone have to be quite before I send you to yo room," Officer Simms demanded.

 "Okay, I'll be quiet," he boy responded in his natural tone.

The boy sitting on the right side of him, asked if he was alright.

"Yes, um okay," he answered as his eyes focused back on the movie.

"The evil is coming!" the boy says again. This time screaming at top of his lungs, and then he begins to shake as he stood up repeating it over and over. "The evil is coming! The evil is coming!"

Every time he says it, his voice gets deeper and louder. The boys in the dayroom are in shock. They begin to move away from the freighting boy as he continued to display bizarre behavior. The officers suddenly cut on the dayroom lights and walked closer to the boy to see what was taking place.

When Officer Sims looked at the boy's face, he saw that his pupils were the shape of snake eyes. The boy was out of control. They begin to try to get control of the boy. He was now in a full rage. His eyes rolled back and forth in his head as he falls to the middle of the floor and went into full body convulsions. The other residents eyes are filled with terror as they witnessed this boy spin out of control. The doors down the hall way begin to shake, as if someone was trying to open them. Then it sounded like someone was banging and kicking on the doors, but no one was in the rooms.

Back in the dayroom the officers attempted to grab a hold of him, however he was way too strong for them.

"Get your handcuffs," one of the officers called out.

The two officers struggle to place the hand restraints on the boy. "Turn him over!" Officer Simms ordered.

The other two officers turn him on his back. They grab his hands and put them behind the boys back. Then, Officer Simms places his cuffs on his wrist. For a moment, the movement stops. The TV which was off, came on and suddenly displayed static. The lights in the dayroom begin to flicker off and on rapidly and furniture begins to move across the room all on it's on. The dayroom is filled with screams. The residents run down the hall to escape the horror of the dayroom.

"The evil is present. The evil is with us," the boy roared as thick liquid ran out of his mouth, then it ran down his shirt. Suddenly, he breaks the hand cuffs without notice. He begins to throw the officers off him like rag dolls. This boy was more than just strong, it was like he had powers from another source. The boy's voice was very loud, deep and demonic. The sound pierced right through your very soul.

As he scrambled about the floor, the color of his eyes changed to a pure white and looked to be deep in his sockets. He paused for just a moment stuck out his discolored tongue and flicked it like a snake. There was an evil presence, so strong even the room temperature changed. Officer Johnson begins locking all residents down to keep them from harm or danger. Within a matter of seconds all the residents were cleared and locked down. The officers stepped back looking in amazement, not knowing what to do. Officer Johnson panics and runs down the hall seeking cover.

"What the fuck!" said Officer Simms backing to the wall, looking in disbelief. All the officer's eyes were wide open with their mouths hung open, as a presence seemed to take over the little boy.

"It's the evil force! It's the evil force!" the demon driven boy roared. The boy then reached out with both his hands, fingers spread apart, wrapped his hands around his throat and begin to violently choke himself.

"Help me! Please help me!" he boy pleaded as his hands gripped his own throat tightly. His fingers sink deep into the skin of his neck. His blood begins to ooze out of his nose. The boy screams for help again, as if he is trying to save himself from himself. The whole room seemed like it's was spinning in a whirl wind. The officers were covered with sweat from all the movement and the unusual blazing temperature of the room.

He continued choking himself, yet begging for help. The officers rushed towards the boy, attempting to remove his death grip from his neck. His tongue hangs out of his mouth, as the foam and spit flies into the air. He turns his head uncontrollable side to side, with his hands still clinched upon his neck. The veins in his forehead begins to protrude, while his teeth grit together tight as vise grips.

"He's too fucking strong!" one officer says, as he tries to remove his hands. The demon boy is breathing heavy and deep. The boys' eyes suddenly turned red as fire. Then he shouted, "get the fuck off me!" in a demoniac tone.

"Stop trying to kill yourself!" another officer cried out to the boy. Then one officer grabbed the possessed boy legs, while two others attempted to remove his hands from his throat. For a moment, the dayroom goes completely dark. Then Officer Johnson reappeared approaching the boy slowly, with wide eyes. All of a sudden, the boy stops all movement and looked directly into Officer Johnson's eyes and tells him, "you opened the pits of hell... you will suffer forever and ever, you bastard!"

Then the demon boy begins to laugh in a deep bottomless tone. The tone of his laughter was demoniac and desolate. His face was discolored and his breath reeks the smell of spoiled death. The sound bounced off the walls and seemly down throughout the halls. Another voice arises through the demon voice. The boy then started speaking in another language. It sounds like a group of people all speaking at once. This was a tongue that was unknown to man. The stench of death flowed from his mouth. The smell alone was enough to make one throw up. The lights in the dayroom went completely dark once again. The TV came on, but there was no volume.

The dayroom was totally out of control. The residents were in their rooms horrified to death of the commotion unfolding from the dayroom. After what seemed like an eternity to the petrified officers, the boy suddenly stopped moving again. The dayroom lights came on and the TV went off again. It was quiet and the atmosphere stood still.

Suddenly, a childlike voice cries out saying, "help me... please help me," the possessed boy laid on the floor sobbing uncontrollably looking up at the officers.

Right away, two people from the medical staff bust through the unit door, rushing over to the boy and begin to check his vital signs. It was the facility nurse and the physician assistant. By now, the boy was coming too. It was as if he had been knocked out. His eyes rolled all about and were in and out of focus.

"What happened?" he asked, in a low tone. His eyes wondered about, as the staff crowed around him, "um scared," he added.

"You had an episode," the PA replied, as she checked him over. She spoke to him in a loud clear voice.

"Am I going to die?" he asked.

"No. No. You're going to be just fine," the nurse said, in a calm voice.

As the nurse raised the boy's shirt up, they were all dumbfounded when they saw that he was covered with razor cuts all over his chest and back. This puzzled everyone. All over his body were letters, symbols and numbers carved into his skin with precision, "help me," was carved into his chest and "Bobby is here." was wrote on his lower back.

What did this mean and who could have done this to this boy? The nurse, PA and security staff looked at each other in silence. No one had an answer. Nor could anyone make sense of any of it. They knew he didn't write all this on himself. It would have been impossible to. It didn't make sense to them and the TV was going on and off and on, well that didn't make sense either.

The boy looked dazed and confused telling the nurse that he didn't remember anything that happened. He also told the nurse and the PA that he was sitting on the couch watching TV and that's all he remembered.

The staff is visibly shaken up by the boy's episode. They could not understand what happened. None of them had ever witnessed anything like this before. No one spoke a word yet, they all looked at each other in total disbelief, after checking the boy's vital signs, he was taken to the infirmary for further observation.

It was determined that he had a traumatic episode. As far as the scratches on his chest and back, that could not be explained. After the medical staff looked him over, he was sent to a local hospital for further observation.

CHAPTER 24

NO POWER

Two days later, the snow continued to fall out the sky. The city of Atlanta had already deemed it to be a state of emergency. On this day, while the residents were at leisure time, the whole facility lost power. The staff was prepared for this kind of situation, so the officer's immediately placed all juveniles in their rooms without incident. The detention center was on an official lock down. Officer Johnson wasn't bothered by the lock down. It seemed as though he has his eye on a new young nurse. Every chance he got, he was in her face making small talk. Its obvious Officer Johnson has the hots for her.

The officers got the power generator going, which was located behind the kitchen. The generator would only hold power for about four days. They figured by then, the power would be restored. For them there wasn't much to worry about. They also broke out the flood lights and emergency flash lights. This was the only source of power they had throughout the whole building. The officers set the three flood lights on each hall and two in the dayroom, where they would be assuming post.

Knowing that the generator would be good for only four days the staff next priority and biggest task was to make sure that if the generator did go out, they would have enough supplies to survive until things were back too normal. They felt that things would be all clear in a matter of days.

Now that the power was down, central control was also down. The security staff pulled the emergency keys, so they could have easy access throughout the whole facility. Because of the location of the building, which sat on a 20 ft. slope and because all of the snow, no one could come in or leave out. The staff knew due to the weather, it was too dangerous for any emergency rescue team to give them a helping hand. In the meanwhile, all the staff could do was hope for the best and try to keep everyone safe and secured. One night while Officer Johnson was making his 30 minutes checks, he decided to go to medical hoping to see the nurse he was interested in. When he got to medical he saw that she was there all alone. He asked her, where was the other medical staff? The beautiful lady told him that everyone else left before the storm moved in. She also told him her name was Nurse Miller. He was delighted to be in her company.

When the call was made for the residents to be on emergency lock down, the boys weren't happy, but then again they understood the nature of the decision. Besides, they had no choice. The dayroom was quiet, no banging on the doors, no rapping, nothing but dead silence. It was so quiet you could hear a whisper. The officers didn't know what to make of the still quiet atmosphere. This kind of silence was very unusual for these juveniles. Never the less, security staff still had a job to do, so they did just that. They did their security rounds and fed the kids, from their rooms of course. For what it was worth, at least everyone had plenty of items to make sandwiches. The items consist of peanut butter, jelly, fruits and all kinds of cans goods that didn't require refrigeration. And lots and lots of bottled water.

In the dayroom, the staff begins to discuss their frustrations about the situation they were in. Some complained that they should have stayed home, while others struggled to stay focus and positive. Indeed, this was a tough position for the staff to be in. It seemed like they all was at their breaking point.

After what seemed to be an eternity of confinement, the juvenile's boredom begins to sit in. As you know, juveniles will be juveniles. So, the boys started making up things to do too occupy their time. Needless to say here comes the noise. The banging, the rapping and all the other things they know to do to get under the staff skin. They did it. And yes, including cussing them out and just acting a fool.

Tony went as far as to learn how to pop the cell room doors. At night, while the staff were sleeping he would pop his door and let a couple of his buddies out. They would grab the officers flash lights and get into all kinds of mischief.

One night, Tony laid in his bed with his eyes wide open. He could not go to sleep. It was very quiet this particular night. Finally, after some hours of tossing and turning, he began to fall into a relax state then into a deep sleep. Tony began to see visions in his dream. Of all people, he begin to see visions of Bobby Berry. The boy he killed some months earlier. Tony's vision was of Bobby going home, walking out of the detention center into the world of freedom. In his vision Bobby was happy. He was at peace. He was free with a big smile on his young face. Tony saw in his dream that Bobby was at home, running and playing in his front yard, like a child is supposed to do without a worry in the world, but it was only a dream.

When Tony woke up, he had a very uneasy feeling about the dream. To him the dream felt real, as a matter of fact a little too real. It was something about it, it just felt strange like it was something more than just a dream. His heart pounded against his chest and sweat poured down his forehead. As he sat up in his bed puzzled, his eyes glazed into the darkness of confusion. He reflected on the incident that took place in the shower that night, some time back. Suddenly, he was consumed with guilt and sorrow.

The following day, Tony didn't tell anyone about his dream. He just tried not to think about it, but the thought of Bobby was heavy and strong on his mind. He couldn't escape it. That night he didn't want to go to sleep, so he did everything he could do to stay awake. He exercised in his room until he couldn't move any more. He started pacing the floor until he got bored. The night dragged by slowly and as it did, Tony wore down. He did all the fighting he could do until his eyes become heavy as stones. Early in the a.m. his body relaxed, he then surrendered to sleep.

Tony slept late into the afternoon skipping breakfast. Much to his surprise he had a good night sleep. No dreams, no tossing and turning. Just good sound sleep. For the next two nights, he slept well. No dreams about Bobby. No bad dreams at all.

The following night, as Tony fell into a deep sleep he begins to dream. He sees Bobby again in his vision. He appeared to be home with his mom, running, playing and carrying on as, if he was care free. This was really strange, because it's the same dream he had some nights ago. The same exact dream.

He was dreaming Bobby was running in his front yard. He suddenly stops and with cold blooded eyes stared at Tony. It was a freighting cold stare. One that he has never felt before. Then in the dream Bobby asked, "why did you kill me?"

Tony quickly woke up in a cold sweat, his heart beating hard and fast. He threw the covers off him, as he sat up in his bed. He wiped his forehead with the palm of his hand. "Fuck!" he said, staring into the night. His voice echo's off the four walls. His eyes opened wide shifting about his room, he's breathing hard and heavy. His room was quiet and unmoving. As Tony gazed into the deep darkness of his room. He had the eeriest feeling that someone was watching him, then he saw Mr. Michael sitting up in the corner of his room. The doll held a slight evil crack of a smile. His eyes seemed to look right through Tony. The boy looked at the doll and thought to himself, how in the hell that doll get in my room? He then walked over to the puppet in placed a sheet over its head, covering it up. He felt a presence, but it wasn't just any presence; no this presence he felt was evil. He begins to feel like something was weighing him down. For the moment, Tony tried to move, but was unable to. Suddenly the hold he felt was gone. He jumps up out his bed, runs to the door and he begins to bang, calling out for Officer Johnson to come to his room for help. The call goes unheard. His heart pounds within his chest. He can feel his blood rushing to his head, making him feel like he was going to faint at any second. His breath was short and his eyes were open wide.

"I must be fucking tripping," he said to himself, with his back against the room door as his eyes scanned the room. Moments later, Officer Johnson walked by his room. Tony got the officer's attention and told him what happened. The officer laughed and said, "yeah. Y'all niggas losing y'all minds in this muthafucka."

The officer then opened his door and shined his flashlight in the room. Tony told the officer that Bobby's doll was in his room. Then he walked over to the puppet and pulled the sheet, but there was no puppet. This further puzzled him. It also frighten him even more. This didn't make him feel any better about being in his room. Maybe I am losing it, he thought. He asked Officer Johnson for permission to sleep in the dayroom and he allowed him.

The following day, the officers agreed to allow the residents to come out of their rooms, as an incentive to behave at night. The residents were very excited about this little reward. While in the dayroom, Tony told Larry all about the dreams he has been having about Bobby.

Larry thought it was funny and said to him, "why you tripping? It was just a stupid dream."

"Yeah. You right," he replied with a smile.

Before long, the sun was beginning to go down and the dayroom was getting dimmer by the minute. The emergency lights were beginning to glow, before long the residents were locking down in their rooms and the full moon was shining bright.

This night Tony paces the floor, like a nervous father in a delivery room. After some time of pacing he decided to lie down and put his feet up. For some reason, Tony just didn't feel right, to him something felt out of place. He couldn't put his finger on it, but he just knew something wasn't normal. He didn't even feel like giving the J.D.O.'s any problems. Plus, he knew that if he did give them any kind of issues, he wouldn't be able to come out his room. So, he laid in bed and tried to relax. He closed his eyes and tried to get some rest, but he was worried about the crazy dreams he had the previous nights. Several hours passed before he fell asleep.

As the morning came, daylight breaks. The grounds are still filled with snow and the skies are silent, to the promise of temperature change. The security staff allowed the residents to have some time out of their rooms. There wasn't much for the juveniles to do. The power was off, but they didn't care. They was just happy to come out their rooms.

Tony and Larry had a chance to talk, for some reason Larry just didn't seem like himself. He seemed to be bothered by something. He was also very quiet, he didn't say much. When Tony asked Larry what was the matter, he stated that he was cool and assured him that everything was okay, but Tony knew better. He knew something was up. He continued to pry. Larry peered expressionless pass Tony, as if he wasn't there. His eyes were empty. The tone of his voice was flat, as he finally told Tony that he had the same dream that he had.

"What you talking bout man?" Tony asked, looking uneasy.

"The dream you had of Bobby Berry- I had that same exact dream last night," Larry whispered with scared eyes.

"That's impossible!" Tony replied, moving closer to him.

"It was just a stupid dream. You remember you told me that?" Larry added.

"Yeah... I did say that, but trust me that was more than just a dream," Tony said slowly. Then he paused and said, "it meant something- what the hell is happening?"

A cold chill ran down Tony's spine. He was suddenly over taken by fear and anxiety. His heart rate increased and his mouth became dirt dry. The boys decided they would talk later on. Neither wanted to talk about these dreams any longer.

Later on the same night, Tony went into his room and went straight to sleep. A fun day of checkers and card games must have worn him out. That night was a very quiet night. Tony slept like a newborn baby. His night was peaceful. Larry also slept well. Neither complained about any nightmares or anything else. They both had a quiet night of good rest.

Some nights later, after a fun filled day of hanging out in the dayroom. Tony returned to his room, with a weary mind. Before long, he fell into a deep sleep. He begins to have yet another vision. He sees Bobby at home, running and playing in the front yard. It seemed as if, he didn't have a worry in the world. In this dream, Bobby suddenly stop at once and stared at Tony with cold bloodied void eyes and asked, "why did you kill me?" Tony's eyes suddenly opened wide. He quickly sat up in his bed then looked around his room. Once again, his room was quiet, then a whisper filled the night air asking, "why did you kill me?"

This time Tony realized that he was not dreaming. "Who was that?" he spoke with a trembling voice. But there was no answer. He went to his door and begin to call for an officer. Officer Johnson responded to his call. He could see that Tony was visibly shaken up, so he allowed him to sleep in the dayroom that night.

Over the following nights, Tony found comfort in sleeping the dayroom with Officer Johnson's permission. In the dayroom, he felt at peace and slept like a new born baby. After a few days, the other officers said he had to sleep in his own room. Tony was very reluctant, but he did as the officers told him.

When he returned to his room the door was already open. He went in and didn't think much of it. As he walked into his room he noticed something that looked to be out of place. He saw that his sheet had been thrown on the floor. What was strange to him was, when he left his room some days ago, and his bed was made and his room was clean. He just figured maybe the security staff may have done a cell search in his room.

As the evening turned to night, Tony laid down to get some rest. Although his mind was unsettled his body shut down from fatigue and sleep gets the best of him. Before he knew it, he was in a deep state of sleep. And before long he begins to dream.

In his dream, he sees a boy in the front yard on a swing. The boy on the swing has his head down. In his vision he couldn't tell who this mysterious boy was.   This boy appears to be swinging in slow motion. It seems to be a hot summer day. The boy swings and he begins to chant, "you can't kill me, um already dead." Tony begins to kick in his sleep trying to wake up. His arms and legs flop about. As much as he tries to fight to wake up, he can't. He was trapped in his own sleep.

The boy in the dream continues to chant as he swings back and forth in slow motion. "You can't kill me, um already dead. You can't kill me, um already dead."

The sound of the chant was a high pitch and piercing enough to make your skin crawl, like someone was scratching a chalk board. The boy repeated this chant several times. As the demonic dream unfolds, Tony struggle to free himself of the horrifying nightmare. He is trapped and locked in this irreversible illusion. As he tries to open his mouth to holla and scream for help, the horror of the night snatch his voice away into the night of the air. As his body jerk his breathing deepens and sweat covers the sheets. His mouth widens but nothing comes out. His eyes flicker as he fights to awake.

In his vision, black crows suddenly appeared. Immediately, the clear blue summer sky disappears. Darkness then falls upon the skies. The bright sun turns blood red. Then it begins to bleed, as if someone had taken a razor sharp knife and cut it wide open. Lighting crackled behind the boy, but there was no rain. The sound of the thunder was loud and heart wrenching, then un-faced boy in the swing abruptly stop in mid swing slowly raised his head, then the face of death, horror and gore appeared. It's the badly beaten face of no other than, Bobby Berry. His eyes held a bottomless empty stare. Still fighting to wake up from this hellish dream, his sheets were soaking wet, as they cascaded to the floor. It was like time stood still, every motion was slow motion.

For a moment, Bobby sat in the swing motionless staring back at Tony. His eyes fixed, both of his hands were still tightly gripped on the ropes of the swing. His eyes rolled back in his head then turned black as midnight. He sits in total silence, tears of blood roll down his cheeks. His face and head is disfigured. His lips are blue like he had been frozen in time.

"Why did you kill me?" he called out in a deep loud shaking voice. As he opened his mouth, blood poured from his lips onto his t-shirt. Tony was then released from this nightmare of hell.

Tony wakes up in total panic. His gray t-shirt was soaking wet. His heart is racing beating in his chest like a drum. Suddenly the sound of footsteps runs across the floor of his room, followed by a child's laughter. His head quickly turns to the direction of the sound. He gasps for air, trying to catch his breath as his eyes stare into the darkness. He is utterly petrified. Tony sit's up in his bed for a moment, he finds the strength to get up and run to his door yelling and screaming trying to get someone's attention. He bangs on the door. Then he tries to pop the lock, but the door wouldn't bulge. Tony stood at the door weeping uncontrollable. His fears, his terrors, his nightmares were becoming his reality.

Much like the times before Tony and Marcus sat together, when they were allowed to have some free time out their room. Tony shared the reign of horror he had experienced the night before. Much to his surprise, Marcus stated that he had the same exact nightmare. He looked in disbelief. Confusion was expressed all over Tony's face. Now things are starting to get downright strange the two boys thought.

Marcus explained how he heard the footsteps running across his floor, his radio has been calling out his name sometimes even trying to talk to him, with the same chants in his dream.

Marcus begin to sing, "you can't kill me um, already dead."

Tony immediately covered his ears and pleaded for him to stop singing that song and to never sing it again. Speechless, the two boys just looked at one another. The two realized that indeed that something wasn't right. How could it be possible that three different people can have the same exact dream? Wow! Tony, Marcus and Larry have all had the same dream. This was something more than just a coincident. Some paranormal things were happening and no one could explain any of it.

That night, Tony and his crew were scared to go into their rooms. The boys begged for permission to sleep in the dayroom, but the officers agreed that they needed to sleep in their own rooms, like everyone else. So reluctantly, they drugged themselves to their rooms for the night.

The thunder and lightning continued to light up the Georgia skies. The sleet crushed against the stainless steel window panes and the thunder continued ripping through the Georgia skies. To make matters worse, they still had the snow to deal with. This was the most unusual snow storm ever. Rain, sleet, snow and thunder you name it. This storm had it.

Tony was determined to stay awake all night and not go to sleep until the morning time. His plan was to stay up all night and sleep all day. He felt this would help him avoid having any bad dreams. So, he did everything he could do to keep from falling to asleep.

The night drugged by slowly. It felt like every second was ten minutes and every ten minutes was an hour. Early in the a.m. about 3:00, Tony eyes started to become very heavy. When he felt like he was losing his battle with sleep, he quickly wobbled to his feet and walked around his room. Sometimes even doing some jumping jacks to stay alert. He looked at his Sony Walkman wishing that it would work, but the

batteries were dead a long time ago. Tony sat on his
bunk, the next thing you know and without warning
he was in a deep sleep. By now it was about 3:45 in
the a.m. He couldn't fight any more. He quickly
became a victim of sleep.

As he slept, illusions of Bobby begins to dance in his
head. He sees a boy swinging. He started singing and
the vision is in slow motion again. The boy swings
back and forward gripping the ropes of the swing
tightly. Slow, slow motion and singing that taunting
chant, "you can't kill me, um already dead."

Tony abruptly opens his eyes. He frantically
awakes to the darkness of his room. His eyes scan the
room from side to side. His blood pumping hard
throughout his body.   His fingers clutch his covers
tightly. His heart beating so loud, he thought he could
hear it beating outside his body. The sound of the rain
tapped against his window and it's the only sound that
can be heard. Inside his cell it's silent and still.
Outside of the window sporadic lighting fills the dark
night skies.   Only a glimmer of light from the
emergency light shines through the small window of
his door. Music abruptly bust through his Walkman.
Unable to move, he listened, suddenly the music fade

and silence was present. All of a sudden, "why did you kill me?" came from the Walkman, at full blast. His heart felt like it jumped out of his chest. He remained still, paralyzed by detestation. His eyes still wide open, looking about his cell. It's quite. A creepy quite, almost felt like someone was standing behind him in the dark. Within the darkness of his cell, he notices eyes looking at him from across the room. There was no face. No figure, only a pair eyes staring right at him lurking in the dark. The eyes were white and without color. When the eyes blinked, they disappeared in the darkness, then reappeared when the eyes opened.

"You can't kill me, um already dead," the haunting whisper fills the night air. Tony quickly ducks his head underneath the covers.

"No!" he yells to the top of his voice. He screams again, "no-no. Help. Please somebody help!"

Then something begins to beat him, while he was under his covers. The blows seemed to come for every direction. The louder he screams the heaver the hits come. The blows seemed to get heavier and heavier. For a moment, he wasn't sure if he was awake or just having a sinister dream. The only thing that he was certain of was that he was scared to the brink of death. He gets up and was shaken so badly, he could barely walk. He manages to make his way to the cell door. He peered out the window looking for some help. Any sort of help, but no one was there. For a moment, he bangs on the door and yells, to no avail. Tony was all alone. His only friend was terror and fright. He tried again to pop the lock, but it wasn't working.

Tony begins to try and calm down. After a few minutes, he collects his thoughts.

"No... no, this can't be happening," he says, as he flopped his body on the lower bunk bed. He paused for a moment, then he looked around the quiet dark room. "Fuck- I must be going fucking crazy," he said to himself, thinking his imagination must be getting the best of him.

He got up off the bed and walked over to his stainless steel water fountain. As he begins to drink from the sink, he notices that the water had a very bad taste to it. In fact, the tasted was horrible. He spits the water back into the sink. After he did, he saw that the water was red. There was only a glimmer of light coming though his window, but it was enough to see that it wasn't water coming from his sink. The taste reminded him of the many times he was playing street football and someone accidently hit him in the mouth and it began to bleed. It was the taste of blood. What the hell? He thought, as he repeatedly wiped his mouth with the bottom part of his t-shirt. Indeed it was blood coming out of his faucet. He walked over to his door and called for the first officer he saw, which was Officer Johnson.

"Look! Officer Johnson, I have blood coming out my sink!" The officer peered back at Tony like he had lost his mind. "Um serious, blood was coming out my damn sink- watch this," he says, as walk over to the sink and presses the water button to show him. When he pressed the button nothing came out the faucet. He stepped back for a moment, then he pressed the water button once more. Again nothing.

"Man, I know what I saw. Um telling you, blood was coming out that shit," Tony said in frustration.

Officer Johnson paused for a second before he spoke a word. He took out his key and proceeded to unlock Tony's door to get a closer look at things. He stepped into his room and went to the sink and looked in it.

"You see blood?" Tony asked, standing next to his bunk.

"Aint no damn blood in yo sink," he said without concern, as he walked out slamming the door behind him. The boy offer no explanation.

First the crazy dreams, then the whispers and now blood flowing out of the faucet. Now this is really starting to worry him, because he knows that something was wrong.

Later that night, Officer Johnson spent half an hour talking to Tony in his room. He talked to the boy until he fell asleep.

The next morning, Tony wakes rather early despite not getting a good night rest. On this morning, the sun seemed to shine extra bright. As he lay in his bunk, his mind pondered on the events from last night. He didn't know what to think about all the crazy stuff happening. He noticed something strange, it was something very strange. Here it was in the middle of winter and his room was hot. Hot to the point where he was sweating and he was starting to feel very uncomfortable as his eyes locked on his wall. He saw that there was some sort of writing on it. The writing wasn't graffiti. It wasn't like the kind you usually see in jail. No, this writing had a message. A very disturbing frightening message. Tony gazed at the writing, as the feeling of butter flies danced in his stomach. Fear instantly filled his heart. The writing on the wall read, "um coming back for you!"

Frighten, he got up to get a closer look. Suddenly blood begins to leak from the walls. Tony takes a step back and looks with disbelief. The blood slowly drips from the writing. The wall then cries out with moans. It's the sound of people being tortured. Cries fill the air, coming out the pits of inferno, begging for the release of their souls. The blood was slowly dripping onto the floor. Something outside his window drew his attention away from the wall, but only for a moment. As he glances beyond his window, he noticed a black crow sitting on the electric line. The black crow had red eyes that shined like a set of rich rubies. The bird seems too stare directly at him, as to be reading his mind. It quickly flew away. When he turned back to look at the wall, he noticed that the walls are no longer bleeding. The walls are clear again, as if nothing was there before. He glances back at the snowy clouds. He begins to weep and scream aloud, "what is happening to me?" he says, looking up at the ceiling.

As the darkness begins to lie upon the facility, night time is quickly approaching. Over the last past days, Tony has been communicating with his sidekick Marcus. The two have been getting together talking whenever Tony could pop his door. If that didn't work, they would talk through passing letters. The boy's rooms are right across from each other. The two boys would often write to each other and slide the letters under the door. This is called Cadillacin. Tony was telling him all about the blood in the fountain and the writing on his wall. With everything that Tony has told him, Marcus knew that they are experiencing the some kind of paranormal activities.

CHAPTER 25

NO PLACE TO GO

It's been weeks since the storm blew in and it seems like forever since the power outage. For Tony, Marcus, Larry and Patrick the weather and the power outage is the least of their worries. So many things have happened; they now feel as though something or someone is after them, even trying to kill them. They didn't understand what could be trying to kill them, but one thing they know for certain is the only way out alive is to escape from this locked down hellhole. The boys make their mind up to escape, somehow, some way.

Marcus lay in his bed eyes wide open. The night has grown late and sleep is all too evasive to him. His heart is heavy, yet his mind is full of thoughts of the role he played in the violent murder and his memory will not let him rest. The shower scene must have played in his head a million times over and over. To Marcus sometimes, it all seemed like just a bad dream and needless to say. He wishes it was.

As his thoughts take him beyond the four corners of his wall, his thinking is suddenly interrupted by something he sees laying in the dark of his room. It's something that appears to have a human form. Instantly, his heart start to race, his eyes widen trying to make out what this human like figure could be. Whatever it is, it's eyes were staring back it him.

"Who is that!" he frantically calls out into the night thin air.

No words are spoken back. Then he hears breathing. Heavy breathing. Whatever it is, it is now floating in the corner of his room. It's human like head almost touching the ceiling. Its red eyes locked on Marcus. His chest tightens like he was about to go into cardiac arrest. The air seems to be getting thinner by the minute. Marcus can barely breathe. Full panic mode begins to sit in. When he catches a glimmer of the light, the real horror unfolds. The shallow light reveals a demoniac fiend elevating in his room. The boy yells and screams as loud as he could, as his eyes widen and sweat pour down his head. As he did paralysis took full control of all his muscle movements. Without warning he was paralyzed by sure terror and fear. This was only the beginning of his living hellish nightmare.

He tries to fight to move, but his breath becomes shorter and by the second. His cries echo off the walls into silence. The demon slowly ascends from the ceiling stretching its' human like arm out toward Marcus. As it does his lips begin to quiver and his whole body is shaken with fear. He felt like his heart was going to stop or explode!

The demon released a groan from the depths of hell. The demoniac figure begins to call out to Marcus, "come to me Marcus- child come to me."

The demon's tone was evil and deep. Marcus stomach rumbles as he muster up the strength pushing himself off his bunk bed falling to the floor. Just as he did his stomach rumbles once more. This time his bowels loosen, running down his pants leg. The stint hits the air which smelled like that of rotten death. Marcus attempts to crawl to his door to free himself of this evil demon. His strength is all but depleted, yet he continued to fight for his last breath.

It was like he was climbing up a steep hill. He crawled around on his hands and knees. It seemed like he was frozen in time, but he pushed the door looking back at the thing that was calling for his soul. The demon begun to speak in different tones, different

voices all at the same time. It sounded like a group of
ten people or more all speaking at once, but one voice
amongst the sound stood out. It was the sound of his
mother's voice, which she had been dead for three
years. The sound of her call was clear unlike the other
voices. Her call was clear, yes clear as a bell and
Marcus recognized her voice, but he kept moving
towards the door. To him it felt like the closer he
moved to the door, the further the room widens
pushing the door further and further away out his
reach.

With all that is happening, he manages to get on his
feet and wobble to his door. He begins pushing and
banging on the door at the same time. His voice
weakens. "Help, help me!" he calls frantically and
repeatedly looking over his shoulder. The door is
locked. It won't bulge, but he continued to beat and
kick the door.

Behind him, the lights in his room begin to flicker off
and on creating a stroll light effect. He slowly turns
toward the dancing lights, as he does he can feel the
tightness in his chest getting stronger. This sends an
unbearable pain through his whole body. With both
hands he clutches his chest, as he grits his teeth

together. He can also feel the room filling with pressure, which is making it difficult for him to breathe.

"Hey! Are okay in there?" a familiar voice call to him from the other side of the door.

Marcus quickly turns around, now looking out his door. "No! Please let me out, it's a demon in here!" he yells.

Suddenly his eyes connect with the voice of the person on the other side of the door. He can't believe what he sees. It's Bobby. Bobby Berry was standing outside his door, looking right through his eyes into his soul. Bobby cracks an evil smile, as his piercing eyes remained locked on Marcus. If Marcus could cry, he would, but the terror was beyond tears. It was beyond anything imaginable.

"No! No!" he yells over and over.

The room temperature turns up and then turns up again. The mattress on the bunk begins to shrivel like a plastic bowl, in a microwave oven. Marcus's room is like that of an oven. Sweat pours from his body like a running faucet. His skin begins to bubble from the intense extreme heat. Blisters begin to form over his arms, neck and face. As the heat intensifies, his feet starts to melt and begins to stick to the floor, like a slice of cheese pizza fresh out the oven. He tries to run to his bunk, in attempt to get off the scorching hot floor. As the pressure continued to fill the room, his body was already blistering. Now, his head begins to swell like a balloon, being blown up by a helium tank. As his head expanded, his left eye bulges out its' socket almost hanging out.   His face is suddenly covered with blood. His pain is unbearable. His yells and cries are confined only to his cell.

Marcus is now at the mercy of Bobby Berry. As his skin rips, blood flows out his face partially exposing his facial bones and muscle beneath the skin. Bobby begins to laugh in a deep devilish voice, as he unleashes his torture beyond one's imagination.

Marcus head continues to swell bigger and bigger. Both his eyeballs suddenly pop out of the socket it. His head then explodes sending brain matter all over the walls and floor of his room. His body collapses to the floor like a ten pound weight. His body is headless and life less. He goes into a full body convulsion. The middle of his floor opens up sending his body into the bliss.

CHAPTER 26

THIN AIR

"Did you hear about what happened to Marcus last night," Officer Johnson asked, with a slumber look on his face as he was standing at Tony's door.

"No, what happened to him?" Tony asked, with concern.

"We found blood, brains and all kinds of crazy stuff in his room this morning. But there was no body," Officer Johnson said.

Tony suddenly stood to his feet. "What the fuck are you talking about? I just talked to him last night!" he added. There is a long quiet pause.

"I'm sorry," Officer Johnson said, dropping his head in despair.

"Man what you talking about. That's my nigga. What happened? How did he die?"

"Don't nobody know. Ain't nobody heard nothing, seen nothing. This shit is crazy," said Officer Johnson.

"That's fucked up!" Tears swelled in his eyes. Then there is a long silence.

"This place is haunted!" Tony yelled.

"No shit," Officer Johnson said, with authority.

"Me and Marcus have been having a lot of crazy dreams."

"Dreams? Dreams about what?" Officer Johnson interrupts.

"Crazy shit!" said Tony.

"Crazy shit like what?" Officer Johnson asked.

"Well... like twice, two times. You know what I'm saying? Me and cuz had the same exact dream. It was about that nigga Bobby."

"Bobby? For real!" Officer Johnson said, looking confused and surprised at the same time.

"Hell yeah. That shit was scary as fuck, shawty... for real. I think he's coming back to get us. And I think that's what happened to Marcus, on some real shit."

"Damn!" Officer Johnson says. At that moment, he seems to be at a loss for words.

"Johnson, we have to get the fuck out of here. He ain't finsta kill my ass."

"Tony, where the fuck we gone go? How you gone even get out? This shit is locked down," Officer Johnson said.

Tony then sat on his bed, as if he was thinking of a master plan.

"Officer Johnson. Officer Johnson!" a voice yelled out from down the hallway behind him.

"Hold tight. Be right back," Officer Johnson says, to Tony as he exists the room locking the door behind him.

"Who called me?" Officer Johnson calls out in the hallway. No one replies.

Officer Johnson asked again, "anybody call for me?" This time a few boys appeared in their windows looking out.

"What going on?" a boy from another cell asked.

"Somebody called my name a second ago?" Officer Johnson said.

The boys in the window all said the same thing.

"Nobody called you."

Ya'll need to stop playing with ya'll bad asses. Officer Johnson thought to himself. Then he turned around and went back to Tony's room. Just as he got to Tony's room and begin to unlock his door. The voice called out again.

"Officer Johnson!"

The voice was loud, clear and crisp with a sense of urgency. As if it was an emergency. The voice was so loud, it caught Officer Johnson's attention immediately. Startled, he ran over to the room where he heard the command. He looked inside the room and the room was empty. A chill ran down his spine. He broke into a cold sweat. He peered into the room again. His eyes shifted from one side to the other. He confirmed for himself, the room was empty. This puzzled him, because he knew that someone was calling his name from that room.

Meanwhile, back in Tony's room, he is disturbed about the news he heard about Marcus. It is now night time. Once again, sleep is evasive. He's up and down all night pacing the floor. His heart weights heavy. Not only was he disturbed about Marcus, he was petrified that Bobby was going to get him next. So, Tony felt he had to talk to Larry and Patrick. He wanted to see, if they had heard about what had happened to Marcus. He wanted to know, if they heard or seen anything else strange. He decided to break out his room and go see Larry first. Like magic, 1, 2, 3, his door was opened. He thinks to himself, these old locks are easy to pop. Tony stuck his head into the hallway, looking both ways. He wanted to make sure the coast was clear. There was no one in sight, at least from what he could see. Then he tipped toed into the dayroom, where he sees an officer laid across the couch and snoring loud enough to wake up a hibernating bear. He sees that no one else is around. He quietly runs down to D hall unit. He gets to Larry's door. He peaked in and saw him still awake. Tony lightly tapped on the door. He shows his face, as to not alarm him. He then popped the lock and entered into his room.

"Man what's up shawty? Fuck you doing nigga?" Larry asks. He has a big smile on his face. He was happy to see his friend.

"I'm straight bruh. Did you hear about what happened to Marcus last night?" Tony asks.

"Naw bruh. What's up?" Larry responds.

"Officer J, told me they found his brains splattered all over his fucken room this morning."

Larry's eyes grew large, as his mouth dropped. "Get the fuck out!" he replied.

"This is some real shit shawty." Tony replied, with a serious look on his face.

"Fuck!" said Larry, as his eyes widened again.

Then Tony went on to tell him, there was no body found. They don't know what happened to his body. Then he filled him in about all the dreams, voices and other crazy things.

Tony asked Larry, has he still been hearing and seeing anything strange?

"Just your ass," Larry said, with an awkward smile. Then he went on to say that he was having bad dreams, dreams about Bobby and also about that doll referring to Mr. Michael. Apparently, Larry has no clue about what he had been going through. He became concerned about what Tony told him. He definitely didn't take Tony's words lightly. As he's engaged in the conversation, Tony tells his story. Larry suddenly sees a dark figure pass by the window of his room. Larry paused, and then he thought maybe it was just an officer doing the nightly security rounds. But minutes later, as he sat and listens to Tony, he sees the dark figure slowly pass by again. The shadow seems to move even slower.

"Look!" Larry yells to his friend.

Tony quickly turns toward the door.

"What!" Tony says, looking frantically over his shoulder.

"Some- somethings out there. Something just passed by my door."

The two then rushed to the door to see what it was. When they looked out the window nobody was there. The hall was quiet. Only a glimmer of light shine from the dimly lit flood lights. The two boys looked at one another, both was at a loss for words. Their hearts fluttered with fear. They quickly dotted back into Larry's room.

"Man this place is fucking haunted," Larry said looking at Tony, as if to say now um convinced. The two boys were shaken up. That night Tony decided to sleep in Larry's room, because he was too scared to go back into the hallway. They both stayed up half the night until sleep took its natural course.

CHAPTER 27

TO BELIEVE OR NOT BELIEVE

Some days passed, before the residents are allowed to come out for leisure time. Talks and rumors swirled about the facility in relation to what happened to Marcus. Most could not believe it or maybe most would rather not believe it. But never the less, this was the perfect opportunity for Tony to talk to his boy's, Larry and Patrick. He told Larry they need to get with Patrick. They need to fill him in and to also find out, if he knows anything about Marcus. They also needed to know, if he has had any crazy unexplained things to happen to him.

Tony hadn't seen Larry in a few days, so he was happy and anxious to hang out with him. Larry told Tony he had been hearing crazy things in his room and not to mention about the shadow they saw while in his room some nights ago. He also expressed to him that he was very afraid for his life, because he felt like someone is watching him all the time while he's in his room.

Tony begins to tell him, they needed to get out of this place, if they wanted to survive. Larry was all the way with it. Now they just had to get Patrick on board.

Later that night while everyone was sleeping, Tony pops his lock and went to Larry's room and popped him out. The group of juveniles begin to put Tony's plan into full swing. Tony and Larry quietly creep up the hall, both boys held flash lights, which they took from an officer sleeping. Tony told Larry that he was going to go to Patrick's room and pop him out. He also suggests that he and Larry split up and of course, as always he agreed.

As Larry turned onto B-hall something strange catches his attention. Out of his peripheral vision, he sees a dark shadow run across the hall into an empty cell. Larry jumps and grab his chest, as if his heart was about to jump out.

"Hey!" he yells down the seemly empty hall. His voice echo's off the walls. He steps in the direction of the faceless shadow with caution. When he gets closer to the door of the room, he sees that the door is slightly open. Larry takes a peek inside the room, then he looks through the window.

The glass is missing, but there is no sign of any broken glass on the floor. As Larry stares through the window, he sees that the room was very dark on the inside. With his right hand, he slowly pushes the door open. As he does, the door squeaked like it hadn't been opened in years. For some strange reason, this door seemed to be much heavier than the other doors, in fact it seem about twenty pounds heavier. Once opened, he slowly disappeared into the darkness.

"Is anyone here?" he said, softly.

His eyes open as wide as he could open them.

"Is anyone here?" he called out again, but this time just a little louder, but again there was no answer.

The night of the room was still and quiet. So quiet, that he could only hear his breathing. Suddenly he hears footsteps running, coming from behind him. He panics and is unable to move. The footsteps get closer and closer. When the steps get right next to him, the steps stop. Larry is shaken with so much fright, he can't run nor can he even move at this moment. Then he feels something breathing down his neck, but no one is there. He quickly turns towards the door. When he does, bang! The door slams on its own. Then the lock turns, locking the boy inside.

Now, he knows he has step into the world of the unknown. The sound of children laughing fills the dark room. First, from the front of the room, then from the back. The laughter is all around him, as if children were running circles around him. In a panic he takes off in the darkness, running in a room he thought to be a cell. But this room was way too big to be a jail cell. It was like he'd stepped into another dimension.

As he looked ahead, he could see a crack of light shining through another slightly opened door. As fast as he could, he ran to the door looked and entered the mysterious room. As he did, Larry could see that this particular room was not dark, in fact it was full of light. He noticed a man at the end of the hall sitting in a wheel chair. The man was all alone. The man in the wheel chair also had an oxygen tank that sat on the floor, to his right side. The man in the wheel chair appeared to be lifeless, but his eyes remained wide open.

"Hey!" he boy called out to the old man in the wheel chair, but he did not respond. "Sir!" he called out once more, but again the man didn't move nor did he say anything.

Then suddenly, as Larry stared at the man the lights begin to flicker on and off. Then the lights went completely out, leaving the boy in total darkness. His heart begins to beat even faster with his eyes widening. The room also was very quiet, as he starts to try to feel his way around in the dark. The lights came back on, but only for a second. When the lights came on for that moment, he could see that the man in the wheel chair was no longer there. The wheel chair was there, but the man wasn't. Suddenly the lights went off once again, but only for a second or two. Low and behold when the lights came back on, Larry adjusted his eyes. He abruptly sees the old man in the wheel chair running toward him in full speed. Frighten, he then begins to back up as fast as he could. His legs felt like they weighted a ton. As the man gets inches away from him, he closed his eyes as he stumbles and falls backwards to the floor. He lies there motionless, balled up with his hands covering his head. Much to his surprise, when opens his eyes there was no one there. He then peered down the hall way, where the wheel chair was. The wheel chair was no longer there. Larry slowly managed to get to his feet and continued down the hall way hoping to find a way out.

On this hall there were six rooms on each side, as Larry begins to walk down the hall he noticed that people were in the rooms. As he walked by the people in the rooms, they started to bang on the doors as to gain his attention. One man stood in his room motionless. His eyes stared into the atmosphere into nowhere. The man across from him walked in circles at a rapid pace. The man uttered jargon, which made no sense. Who are these people Larry thought to himself. In another room, a lady is there her face filled with rage and anger, both her hands tightly balled to a fist, as he walked by. The woman belted every curse word one could imagine. A couple doors down, one person walked back and forth by the door. He couldn't make out if it was a male or a female, but they were saying something, talking to themselves. The voices were loud as he passed the rooms, but then the voices lowered and fell into total silence. Larry turned around and looked again. No one was in the rooms or the hall.

"Hey come here," the sound of a female voice rings out, catching Larry's attention. He turned around and noticed a beautiful woman standing at the door in a room. She was white, had pretty long brown hair and wore a smile that would make any man weak about the knees. She was draped in only a white flowing gown. He slowly walks over to the beautiful young women standing in the door.

"What the fuck is this place?" he asked, watching her closely.

"Oh," said the lady with a big smile, "this is the psych ward."

"The psych ward?" Larry repeated.

"Yes, this is nurse Young's unit," she said.

"Please can you tell me how to get out of here?" Larry asked.

"We are here forever, we will never leave, but you...you can leave. You see that door right there?" The lady in the door paused as pointed in the direction of the door, which appeared to be just at the end of the hall.

"That door will get me out of here?" he asked with a sense of uncertainty.

"Yes!" the lady said, "yes, but you must hurry- you must hurry," she said again.

As the mysterious lady turned around from the door, Larry could see that she had a big hole in the back of her head. The hole was big enough to put a grown man's fist in it. His eyes then drew to the corner of the room and he saw brain matter and blood that was splattered all over the walls. He felt weak, as if he was about to pass out. Just for a moment, his knees buckled, as his stomach turned. It appeared that the mysterious lady had been shot in the back of the head blowing her brains out all over the room. He quickly turns away and runs to the end of the hall as fast as he could.

He pushes the door, it easily comes open. He steps into the dimly lit room. He suddenly steps on a bottomless floor, falling into a pool. Before he knows it, he is up to his shoulders in water. Frighten, he panics and begin to swim for his life. The water is murky, thick and red. It's not water he has falling into. It's a pool of blood.

As he gasps for air, his head dot in and out the pool of blood. Headless bodies and disfigured body parts of the dead float all around him, occasionally bumping against him.   Larry closes his eyes tight, as he continued to fight to get out the pool of horror. When his eyes open, he is suddenly face to face with Bobby Berry.

Bobby grabs his legs then begins to pull him under the thick murky blood as he attempts to swim away. Larry swims to edge of the pool, then begins to pull himself out. But, Bobby is pulling on his legs trying to pull him back into the pool. Larry begins to fight as hard as he could, but Bobby's fight is harder and he is determined to get his revenge by way drowning him.

As Bobby pulls, Larry is starting to lose his grip of the edge slipping back into the pool of condemnation. Suddenly, he manages to break free of Bobby's grip. He gets out of the pool.   He staggers to his feet and begins to run down the hall, which led back to the boys unit.

Meanwhile, back in the dayroom, as Officer Johnson grabs his heavy duty flash light, he pulls his tired body up from the big chair in the dayroom. He takes in a deep breath of air, as if he's standing on the top of a mountain.   As he stood there in the dayroom, something felt very weird to him. Out of place. He had a crazy feeling that someone was watching him. It was a feeling that he had never experienced before. All of a sudden, it felt like someone was breathing on his neck.

Officer Johnson quickly turned around looking behind him, nothing was there. Then he turned around again, still nothing. This shit is crazy, he thought to himself, as he flashed his light all around him and down the stretch of empty hall of each unit. Just as the officer put his flash light down, he hears screaming coming from D-Unit. It startled him. He quickly flashes the light down the hall. "Help me! Help me!" a voice calls out in distress.

"Who is that?" The officer replied shining his light, as he slowly and caution walk down to D unit. He saw a broom stick which had been broken in two. One end was pointed, as if someone had made a jail house weapon. He picked it up for his protection and continued down the unit.

The banging starts, but only for a moment.

"Please! Please! Somebody help me," the voice cries out again.

"Um coming- just hold on," Officer Johnson yells, as he starts to sprint down the hall as fast as he possibly could with flash light in hand.

As he reached the door, the screams went silent. He looked into the dimly lit room. He didn't want to go inside yet. He could feel the beat of his heart kicking like a mule against his chest. At first look, the room was very dim and it appeared to be empty which baffled Officer Johnson. As he continued to move forward, he could see someone walking around in the room. The figure was pacing back and forth slowly. He sees there's also a dark shadow on the wall that followed the figure. The officer could not make out who it was, because the lighting was poor in the room.

"Hey!" he called, "Hey!"

There was no response. Just for a moment, Officer Johnson looked up the hall like he was waiting on the team to come running down to help him out like they usually would, but this time there was nobody. He then turned his attention back on the figure in the room. When he did, he didn't see the shadow or the dark figure. Whoever or whatever it was walking in the room, it was as if they had vanished into thin air. To Officer Johnson, this didn't make any sense whatsoever, because he knew what he had seen with his own eyes.

As he continued to look into the room out of the darkness, the figure reappeared. The unknown figure paced slowly walking back and forth. Then just like before it disappeared in the darkness. He begins to yell through the door, trying to get the attention of whatever it was. He also shines his flashlight into the dimness of the room, but again no one was present.

As Officer Johnson stood there still looking into the room, he lowered his head now looking at the floor contemplating, if he should go inside the room or not. He thought that wouldn't be such a good idea, because after all he didn't know who or what was walking around in there. When his eyes refocused back on the room, there was a loud crash on the window. The room suddenly was bright. It was Mr. Michael. Bobby Berry's lost ventriloquist doll was standing inside the room at the door staring right at Officer Johnson. The evil doll belted the most evil groan from the belly of hell. The head of the doll turns all the way like the head of an owl. Then it throws up yellowish, greenish vomit all over the window. Suddenly Officer Johnson screams at the top of his lungs. Petrified with fear, he jumps back losing his footing and crashes into the cell door across the hall. His eyes were still locked on Mr. Michael, as he struggles to pick himself up off the floor, another voice calls out from the room just behind him.

"Hey Officer J, look at me!" just as Officer Johnson quickly turns to look over his shoulder, a young boy jumps with a sheet tied around his neck. As the boy drops, the sheet tightens. Choking the life out of him. The boy's eyes buck wide open locking on the officer. Blood poured out his mouth and his nose like a leaking faucet. His body jerks, as his neck crack and snap. The sound was loud, like someone stepping on a giant cock roach. The boy toes pointed downward just inches from the floor. His body swings side to side as urine and defecation roll down his leg, dripping on the floor. The stench flowed from underneath the door right into Officer Johnson's nostril and down his lungs. The officer staring up at the hanging boy with his eyes bucked as fear consumed him.

The officer and the boy eyes locked together like they were in a staring contest. The hanging boy was Bobby Berry. He blinked his wide open eyes again and said in an evil whisper tone, "um back Johnson!"

The officer continued to stare in disbelief his mouth hung wide open, suddenly the officer musters up enough strength to get up and run for his life like he never ran before. As he sat in dayroom trying to get himself together, he saw nurse Miller in the control room, but he was just too messed to even try to talk to her. At this point, the only thing that Officer Johnson is really interested in is getting the hell out this place.

CHAPTER 28

CANT TAKE IT ANYMORE

As the days passed and the snow continues to turn to ice, some of the staff members begin to lose their composure. The reality starts to set in that they might not make it through the storm alive. Some of the members even begin to act like they were losing their minds. Especially Officer Johnson. His conscious was playing guilt trips on him, because he knew he was part of an innocent boy becoming a victim of death.

Officer Parker notices that Officer Johnson was acting strange and jumpy. It seemed like every time he heard a sound he would just about jump clean out his skin. He begins to talk sporadically and really crazy from time to time. He was always talking about Bobby Berry and that puppet. It seemed like he was losing it. At this point, Officer Parker and the others was concerned about him.

Officer Parker knew how important it was to keep everybody together. And if anyone could do it, then it would have to be him. But the truth of the matter was, it wasn't just Officer Johnson. It look like they all was starting to unravel.

One day the security staff members was fussing and arguing about who should do what. A loud scream erupts from down the hall of B unit. The screams were loud and disturbing. Three staff members immediately turn their attention in the direction of the screams. They sprint down the hall to B unit to investigate.

Officer Johnson had his flashlight in his hand and was ready for whatever. Once at the door they realized that no one had the keys to unlock the resident door. Officer Simms calls the boy, to get his attention. It appears that he was in a deep sleep. It also appears that he is having a nightmare. A bad one at that. As the officers look into the window, they saw that he was kicking and his arms were flopping all around. They could also see that he was under his covers.

"Wake up!" each staff, yelled out aloud.

"Hey what the fuck is going on?" one resident asked, who was next door looking out his window.

Then suddenly, the other residents faces begin to appear in the windows, from being awaken from all the commotion. The others were trying to see what was going on out in the hallway.

"He ain't waking up!" said Officer Hill, as he turned to his co- workers.

"Officer Johnson, um gone get the keys. You stay here!" ordered another officer.

"I'll come with you said, Officer Hill.

The two officers ran up the hall to the dayroom to get the keys out of the control room. While Officer Johnson kept an eye on the boy, a strange thing happened. The door suddenly flew opened, slamming with a big crash into the wall. Without thinking twice about it, Officer Johnson ran into the room and began to shake the boy. The covers were moving, as if someone was wrestling with him underneath it.

Officer Johnson frantically called out aloud, while shaking him and looking back at the door, hoping that help would arrive soon. Suddenly, the officer yanked the covers off the boy. He is exposed, still kicking and screaming violently with his eyes closed. Then almost at once, he became quiet and still. The boy looked at the officer with strangest look ever. He pointed leading the officer eyes under the bed. When he flashed his light under the bed, he saw Mr. Michael lying on the floor. The officer was alarmed, as he stared at the puppet. What the fuck? He thought. He then moved closer to get a better look. When he did it looked like to him that the puppet's chest was raising and falling, as if it was breathing. As he looks even closer, he could see that the puppet was in fact breathing like it was alive. How could this be? He thought to himself. This can't be possible. As Officer Johnson begins to draw closer to the puppet, it slowly turns its head looking into his eyes. The officer quickly jumped backed with a loud scream at the top of his voice. Then he ran out the room like his life depended on it, leaving the boy in the room.

As he ran out the room and up the unit in terror, Officer Simms met him half way up the hall.

"It's something in that room!" he yelled as he ran, not looking back.

"What?" the officer asked.

"Something's in that room!" Officer Johnson said, once more.

"Something like what?" Officer Simms asked, with a puzzled look on his face.

"Man, I don't know what the fuck it is. Um not going back in there. That fucking doll is in the room!" Officer Johnson said, with fear.

Disregarding what he said, Officer Simms and Officer Parker goes down the hall into the boy's room. The door was still open. The officers walked in slowly. By this time the boy was visually shaken and very scared. He was sitting on his bed crying supporting his back against the wall with his head between his knees.

When the officers asked him what happened and what was wrong? He said with his head down, in a low tone, "he's here. He's here."

"Who's here? Who are you talking about? Was a doll in your room?" one of the officers asked.

But the boy didn't give an answer. He just continued to say, "he's here!" As his brown eyes stared into nowhere.

Officer Simms asked again, "who the hell you talking about?"

"Bobby- um talking about Bobby Berry... he's back." the boy said, as he lifted his head looking into the distance.

The hair on the back of their necks stood up. This sent chills up and down the Officer's backs. The staff was stunned and shaken by what he revealed.

Without another word being said, they collectively all walked out of the room. The officers left him there. Then they went to the control room to regroup and get themselves together.

"I can't take this shit no longer," Officer Hill says.

"What you gone do? You just gone give up?" Officer Simms replies.

"I know this been rough and none of us asked for this shit, but it's the hand that's been dealt to us. Don't lose it, we have to stay strong. We gone survive this shit," Officer Simms said, trying to encourage everyone sitting in the control room.

Officer Johnson begins to cry breaking down saying, "man we all gone die in this place."

The group of officer's all ban together and tried to tell him that they were going to make it out alive. The group sat around eating perishables rations, sardines and sandwiches drinking bottled water. They were eating anything they could find in the kitchen.

The stranded officers can only hope and pray that this terrible snow storm will blow over soon and they all can be saved. But in reality, hopelessness begins to set in. After several months, the snow is still packed against the windows and the wind is still howling like a wolf.

Most nights icicles can be heard breaking and falling off the roof, sounding like someone breaking a stick. Miraculously, one thing that no one seems to be worried about was the heat. Even though it's freezing cold outside, like 5 below Celsius somehow the building remains warm on the inside. But again, the only thing the staff can do is hang in there until the storm moves over.

CHAPTER 29

DRIP, DRIP!

Larry lay in his bed, his mind begins to wonder about his past and his future or if he would even have one. He begins to plan things out in his head. He wasn't really sure what he wanted to do, but one thing was for certain, he didn't want to end up in prison like his older brother. For now the important thing is, he must make it through this storm.

Within minutes, Larry eyes becomes heavy. He is now beginning to doze off and on, falling in and out of sleep. Moments later, sleep gets the best of him.

Drip, drip. Something is dripping on the floor of Larry's room. As it hits the floor, the dripping sound is loud. It's the sound like that of dancing tap shoes. What the hell is that? He thinks to himself rolling over in his bed.

At first, he thought it was the water leaking from the sink. He realizes it's dripping from the ceiling. He rolls back over, trying to continue his sleep.

Several minutes go by, before Larry is fed up with the loud dripping and the tapping sound. Unable to ignore it any longer, he finally gets out his bed to investigate. He reluctantly gets up, walks over to where the dripping sound was coming from. He bends over and touched the floor. He looks at his finger and noticed it was red.

"What the fuck!" he said.

He realized that the dripping isn't water. It is blood. Now, he is confused. He's thinking where in the hell could blood be coming from? As he looked up, he could see that the blood is coming from the ceiling of his room. Larry take two steps back as he looks in disbelief. He wipes his finger on a piece of toilet paper lying near the sink.

Scared, he goes over to his door and begins to scream, kick and bang on the door trying to get one of the officer's attention. But the room is like a sound proof booth. The air catches his breath. No matter how loud he yelled, no matter how hard he kicked on the door, not a word or a sound came out.

After he realized no one was coming to his door, he laid on his bed. He was wishing that the morning would come and save him. As he laid there already shaken by fear, he sees his door slowly opens but no one is there. Then he hears footsteps, as if someone just walked into his room. The footsteps come to his bed, right where he was laying. Then it suddenly stops. He doesn't move. The boy doesn't speak. He is scared and crying, trying not to make a sound. He just lay there not knowing what to do or what will happen next. In the darkness of his room, the walls start to move slowly. So slow, that if you weren't paying any attention you wouldn't realize the walls were moving inward. Larry's eyes pierced each of the four walls, as they begin to turn blood red. Then suddenly, the walls begin to take form of human body parts. Arms, faces and legs begin to protrude out of the walls. His eyes grew even wider, as his heart flooded with fear. Unable to scream or yell he continued to bang on the door, just hoping to get somebody's, anybody's attention.

As he kicked and banged, his eyes shifted focus back on the transforming walls. Larry suddenly felt flames shooting up through his feet. He begins to jump around like he was playing a childhood game of hop-n- scotch. Then, he looked down at his floor, it had turned bright red and orange as a bright sun shining day. The boy felt every bit of the fire. As he quickly hops across the floor, blisters begin to appear on the bottom of his feet.   He ran to his bed for cover, sweating profusely.

Larry took his blanket and covers lying on his bed and covered himself as to hide from the terror.   By now, the wall is in full human form.   The legs, arms and the heads are protruding out of the walls reaching and grabbing for him.   The walls begin to cry out with moans of sorrow and pain.   This wasn't any cry.   These were cries of lost people begging for their souls.   These were the cries and howls from the bottomless pits of hell.   The arms and hands reached out to Larry coming just inches from his face.   Bones protruded though the skin of the arms of the dead, while some of the hands were brunt to a crisp.

The eyes of gloom and doom looked down upon him begging, "save our souls. Save our souls. Please, have mercy on me," a voice rang out from within the walls.

There were many voices all at once. The tone was the same, remorseful and very sorrowful.   Some voices were not understandable to man. It was like a record being played backwards.   And the others, it was the sound of pain, torcher and total abomination. The cries were like no other.

Larry peeked from under his covers. As his body shook, his teeth chattered so hard, that you could hear the sound amongst the moans of the dead. His heart raced and his breathing was shallow. The human like wall moved in what seemed like slow motion. The arms reached out to the boy, as if they were waiting on the frighten boy to grab his hands and pull them out of the walls.

The human figure in the wall was made of muscle only. Some of the eyes on the heads had been gouged out. One of the figures reached out for the frighten boy and begin to call his name. This particular one, its whole upper body stuck out of the wall. It was just inches from him and seem to be getting closer and closer.

Suddenly Larry's eyes opened. He screamed and kicked as loud as he could. Sweat poured down his face. Then the blanket and covers he was holding onto, flew out his hands across the room. He quickly sat up, looking frantically across his dimly lit room. He looks at the walls carefully. Still shaken, he sat for a moment now realizing that he had a horrible dream.

He quickly scans his room again. It's quiet. The glare of the emergency light shine through his room door.

He then uses his gray state issued t-shirt to wipe the sweat still pouring from his face.

"Damn that shit was scary!" he said in a low tone looking dazed. Then he leans over his bed peering into the darkness and underneath his bed. He was checking to make sure nothing or no one was there. He stares for a moment before he sat up in his bed again. He is convinced nothing was there. Then he got out of his bed. He walks over to the sink out of nowhere, Bobby Berry's arms appeared from under his bed. You could not see his face. You could only see the back of his head and his arms stretching out from under the bed. As he looks down, Bobby grabs his ankles then begins to pull him under the bed, into the world of darkness.

He hollers for help, as he falls and hits the floor. He then tries to free himself from Bobby's grip. The more Larry tries to free himself, the more Bobby's sharp fingernails shred through the boy's legs. Within a matter of seconds, Bobby has full control of him under his bed. Larry screams. The screams echoed throughout the room, as he disappeared into eternal darkness under his bed.

CHAPTER 30

HELP ME!

As the night slowly moves on, Officer Johnson and Simms serves as watch duty. A duty that both men would rather had passed on to someone else, but never the less tonight is their night. Both the officers are sleeping heavily in the dayroom, passed out on the plastic couches, with their flash lights at their sides.

Officer Johnson is suddenly awakened out of his deep sleep. He hears alarming screams. The screams were loud enough to shatter a light bulb. The screams are followed by kicking and banging on the door. As Officer Johnson focus to gather himself, his eyes are directed down C-hall unit. For some odd reason the hallway looked so much longer then it usually is.

Fuck! He thought to himself, as he was reluctant to move his tired body. He tried to wake Officer Simms, who was snoring up a storm and he wasn't moving. The banging and kicking noise continued. After trying to wake up the other Officer, with no success, he decided to investigate for himself.

As Officer Johnson walked down the hall, the strange noises increased. "Stop banging on that damn door," he yells out, as he walked down the hall.

"Come to my room!" the voice calls out the officer.

"What the hell you want? Yo ass need to be sleep?" he calls back with his flash light leading the way down the dimly lit hall. As the officer gets closer to the room he could see the door moving. It looked like someone was shaking on the door handle trying to open it.

"Hurry, come fast!" the voice called out frantically.

As Officer Johnson approached the door, the banging and kicking stops. The hall is totally silent. When he gets to the door, he looks inside the room and asks if they was okay? There was no response. He asks again. This time shining his flash light inside the room while looking in. As he looked in the room, he sees that no one appears to be present. The officer takes the butt of his flash light and knocks on the window.

"Hey... who is in there?" he calls out, waiting for a response. His voice echoed down the dark empty hall.

"This shit is crazy," he said looking puzzled as he begins to look inside the other rooms to see where the noise was coming from. He looks back up the hall.

Officer Johnson discovered that all the boys on the hall were fast asleep. Some were even snoring.

Seeing that all the residents was sleeping he didn't know what to think. What the hell? He thought, as he scratched his head.

"Please help me!" a childlike voice called out from the same room again, where the door was shaking. Officer Johnson quickly turned his flash light on the room. He went to the door and took out his keys, which was attached to his key chain. He proceeded to unlock the door. He then stepped inside the room slowly with caution.

"Who the hell is in here playing?" he asks scanning the room with suspicious eyes. Once again, no one answered. Then suddenly the door slammed. He could hear the door locking behind him.

"Oh shit! Help somebody help!" He begins to yell out while pushing on the door trying to unlock it. He knows he is now locked inside the room. He also knows the only one that could help him is Officer Simms, but what was the chance of waking him up? He tried to kick on the door as hard as he could. He yelled as loud as he could for the other sleeping officer, but again there is no response at all.

After several minutes he begins to run out of breath. He tried to calm down and think of another plan. So, he decided to sit on the bed and try to get comfortable relaxing his back against the wall. As he started to gather himself, he heard a loud thump on the door. He suddenly jump to his feet and looks out the door window. He was hoping that someone was out there, to let him out of this room. As he looked out the window, no one was there. He looked in both directions again, nobody was there on the hall.

"Hey!" Officer Johnson called out loudly, "who's there?" he asked.

Then there was the sound of footsteps pacing the floor back and forth, right behind him. He takes his flash light and shine it about the room. As he does, he can see foot prints walking in the room. The prints where as if someone had walked in a puddle of blood. As the officer flashed his light again, there were blood prints all over the floor and walls. Whatever it was, left blood foot prints on the ceiling.

The officer is shaking so hard that he drops his flash light. As it hit the floor, it rolled. He picked it up. He then backed up to the door with his eyes wide open and his mouth just about to drop to the floor. He felt weak in the knees. His stomach flipped.   He felt dizzy in the head.   Then he felt the presence of someone breathing on him from behind. The breathing was so close that he could hear it. He could even smell it, but he just couldn't see anybody. He sensed its presence. This presence was strong. It felt evil.

From the glare of the light, just outside the cell door he could see a shadow on the wall. Then the laughter exploded, followed by singing. It's the voice of kids, as if they were playing on the school's playground. He didn't see any kid's. He only heard the voices singing that all familiar song, "you can't kill me, um already dead." It was repeated over and over.

"No- no!" the officer yelled, trying to cover his ears from the piercing dreadful chant. He dropped his flash light on the floor once again. As he picks it up, out of the dark a nun draped in a full black gown, holding the hand of a young boy appeared right in front of Officer Johnson's face. The nun's face was of skeleton only. The officer falls to the floor, backing himself to the door again yelling and screaming. The nun holding the boy's hand slowly walked toward the frighten man.   Her hands where made of winkles, which look like the hands of a very old person with long black finger nails. The officer noticed that the nun walked with a limp. The boy looked to be about five or six. His face was lifeless. He looked sad and appeared to be desolate. There was no soul in his eyes. As the nun and boy slowly approached Officer Johnson, the nun begin to reach out her right hand to him. The closer the nun got, the louder the officer screamed and kicked. Just as the nun and the boy became within inches away, the door suddenly flew open.

"Man! What the fuck is wrong with you?" Officer Simms asked, looking down at Officer Johnson. When Officer Simms opened the door, he was still on the floor kicking and screaming like he had lost his mind.

"Man get yo crazy ass up off that damn floor," he barked in an angry tone.

Officer Johnson just looked around the room frantically. He was very jumpy. The nun and the boy disappeared into the darkness without a trace. The boy with the nun wasn't a boy at all, it was Mr. Michael, Bobby's dummy.

Officer Johnson was relieved to hear a voice he recognized. He slowly picks himself off the floor and tries to catch his breath. He was so frighten that he couldn't even talk. He had a look on his face that Officer Simms had never seen in all the years they had worked together.   He begins to question Officer Johnson about, why he was locked in that room and what had happened to him. Officer Johnson was still to shaken up to say a signal word. Officer Simms would have never believed the horror that Officer Johnson just witnessed.

CHAPTER 31

DON'T LEAVE ME!

On a night when Patrick is up late and can't sleep he begins to exercise in his cell. A small, but a very bright light shines through a small crack in his room. Curious he slowly gets up on his bed to get a closer look. He could see that a light is shining through his door, but this is very strange because it is much brighter than the emergency lights. This made him want to see, what was going on even more. He slowly rose up and got out his bed, as he approached the door, he pushed it open with one hand.

His heart beat started to increase, as he opened the door wider and wider. Then the door is open wide enough for him to step inside. In his mind he was thinking this just might be a way out. When he stepped inside the lit room there is nothing that he can see, except for a big giant bright light. The boy put both of his hands in front of his face, as to block the high beam of the light. He slowly takes four steps inside the room. Still blinded by the light, he then stops in his tracks. The door slams with a loud crash behind him. Bam!

The loud sound startled him and gets his attention immediately. He turns and faces the door. Then he tried to open the door, but it was tightly locked.

Then he turned around and begins to walk forward through the bright shining light. As he does, the bright light disappeared and suddenly there was a hospital. The lights in the hospital fell dim. Dim to the point where one could barely even see. The room was also filled with thick fog. Patrick begins to hear the moans and cries of sorrow and pain. It sounded like old people. As he proceeded to walk forward, the creepy grim sound became clearer and clearer the closer he got. The hall way also became very narrow on both sides, almost closing him in.

There were beds in the hallway some of them rolled freely and slowly on their own, without any one pushing. And some other beds had, what looked like to be dying patients reaching out for him as he walked by. Some were even touching his face and arms begging and pleading for help. The sounds were of people in excruciating pain and helplessness. It sounded like a room full of people. It was the sound of death and souls being tormented. The smell that filled the room was the stench of death. There were bodies laid around on the floor and in the corners, as if they had been there for years. The smell was foul enough to make you sick to the stomach. As the smell filled the atmosphere, Patrick's nose and his eyes watered. He put one hand over his mouth and the other hand over his stomach, as he walked through this horrific hell hole.

"Please, please... take me with you!" an old man said, walking slowly towards the frighten boy. As he looked at the old man, his shoulders were bloody and the body was headless. It appeared that the head might have been shot off or maybe even cut off. The old man held his own head underneath his arm pit, which spoke for the headless body. The eyes of the head were fixed in a rolled upward position. The mouth was also hung open covered with dried blood. It begins to move saying, "don't leave me!" he repeated it again once more, this time in a much louder aggressive tone.

At the site of this, he begins to run as fast as he his feet would allow him. His knees and legs became so weak, he could hardly stand. He was horrified. As he attempted to run, he staggered and fell. He was feeling like he was in a bad nightmare. His heart beats hard and fast. He fears his legs were almost too weak to carry him. He continued to trip and stubble, as he gasps for air through the endless hall way.

As Patrick looked up, he noticed further down another beam of light shining through the cracks of yet another door. Patrick stood only about ten feet from the door. He tried to run for the door however; his heart was heavy with fear. When the scent of the air hit his nose, it was so bad that he begin to throw up all over the floor. With all the strength in his body, he begins to drag himself to the other partly opened door. The bright light shines through, for he felt nothing could be worse than where he was now.

Once he was at the door he dragged himself inside the room, shutting the door behind him. Inside there was a whole different scene, it didn't smell, and there was normal people grouped closely together just standing around. Who were these people and what were they doing he thought. Patrick could not tell who these people were because they had their backs turned to him. From where he was standing, which was in the back of the room it looked like a church. Suddenly he begin to feel at ease. His breathing slowed down. He slowly and with caution rose to his feet. He wasn't feeling as weak as he was before.

"Hey, hey!" Patrick called from the back of the room. "Hey!" he called out again, yelling. No one from the group moved an inch or even turned around. It was as if no one could hear him calling. Then there was someone standing higher than the others. He appeared to have on a long black robe with a hood that covered his head. He wore a long necklace, with the symbols x36 that hung down to his stomach. The boy had no idea what the symbols meant or who the man was. The sleeves of the robe hung low, so low that Patrick could not see the man hands or his head.

He stared from a distance at the man in the robe. The mysterious man waved his hand to tell Patrick to come to him. The whole time the man's head remained down. As Patrick walked closer, he could see that the people standing around looked like his own family members.

"Mama!" the boy cried out as he stood right next to her. The lady didn't respond. He walked around to where the other people were standing. Then he could see their faces and realized that in fact, it was his family. There his mother, brother and his little sister stood. He begins to scream out each of his family members names. He was trying to gain their attention. No one responded to him, nor did they acknowledge him. He noticed that they were all crying. He continued to look he saw a casket. He looked inside the casket and saw the shock of his life. Patrick saw himself lying in the casket, lifeless. His heart dropped in his stomach. His breathing shut off almost immediately. He felt light headed.

Patrick stared inside the casket with all disbelief. Then the eyes of the dead in the coffin suddenly opened wide. The body is pale and discolored. Its' eyes are red as blood. The casket begins to shake violently rocking back and forth. The upper part of the body wasn't clothed exposing his wide open chest. There were cuts on the chest that read some of syndical message, it said, "Marcus went to hell and you going with him."

The body begins to move, rising up and back into a resting position. Then the dead started to flip back and forth with both its arms stretched out uncontrollably. Howling and screams came from the bottomless abyss, through the mouth of the body. Then after some minutes, the dead body came to a complete rest and suddenly the room fell totally quiet. Just then the body slowly begin to rise up out of the casket. As it floats, the body remained in a laid out position. Then without warning, the body suddenly flew backwards landing crushing hard against the Mosaic window. Shattering it into small pieces of glass. Then the demon spoke to the boy saying in a deep voice, "hell awaits you. Your soul shall perish and burn for all eternity!"

Patrick looks in horror sweating profusely. Then the demon spoke again, "I am you and you are me."

The man in the black robe standing at the casket finished the demon words saying, "and your flesh shall rout in hell!" As he raised his head, reveling its face. It was the face of Bobby Berry. His eyes were black and his pupils were white. He burst into the most cynical evil laugh ever. At the site of this, Patrick's heart was filled with fright. He blacked out passing out on the floor.

It's been some days now, since Patrick has not been able to sleep at night. Just like the rest of the staff and residents he has been doing a lot of thinking as to how he may escape this. This night, he is preparing for bed. He walks over to his bed kneel down to say his prayers. Then he walks to his sink to brush his teeth. He takes a look at himself in the mirror which he don't have much lighting, only a gleam from the hallway. As the boy look at himself in the mirror, behind him he sees a black shadow slowly pass by. He quickly turns around to see what it was. "Who is dat?" Patrick called out into the darkness. His room is quiet. Fear begins to build with in him. He walks over to look out the door to see, if he can see an officer coming his way, but no one is there.

"This shit must be getting to my head," he say's turning to face the mirror again. When he looks into the mirror again, there is a full human like figure standing right behind him. He yells as he quickly turns to face the shadow, but like before there is no one there.

Bang, bang. A knock, rings out loud.

"Oh shit!" Patrick said, as he jumps back from the mirror clutching his chest.

"What's up bruh... you straight?" Tony asks Patrick with a smile on his face. He had popped his door and is running up and down the halls being a mischievous juvenile.

"Man you scared the shit out of me," Patrick said, in a scared voice.

Tony walked down the hall leaving Patrick's door. He watched him as he sneaks down the hall, until he couldn't see him anymore. Just as Patrick turns around there is another loud knock at his door.

"What now?" he asks. When he turned towards his door, his mouth flew open and his eyes just about popped out of his head.

Patrick is in shock to what is at his door. It is a lady standing there with an axe buried in the left side of her face. The lady's left eye is hanging out of the socket and she is drenched in blood from head to toe.

"Help me. Please help," the lady calls out to Patrick trying to enter into his room. His knees buckle. Then he feels light headed. He begins to back away from the door. The old lady continued to bang and scream at his door. Then like a theft in the night, the old lady disappears.

Patrick thinks he is losing it or he is hallucinating badly. After several minutes of getting himself together, he walks over to the mirror again. As he looked into the mirror, he notices something weird about his own reflection. His reflection in the mirror wasn't moving when he moved. When he moved to the right his reflection in the mirror seemed to move slightly slower than he did. When he moved to the left, again the reflection seemed to not move in sequence. Bewildered, he looked in the mirror and moved his head to the right to see if his reflection would move as he moved. Then he leaned his head to the left, but this time the reflection did something different.

The reflection in the mirror didn't move, but only stood still looking back at him. Then it give him an evil smile. He stood before the mirror looking at himself in disbelief. The boy couldn't understand what was going on. To him this didn't make any sense. The boy paused for a moment, as if he was examining the reflection in the mirror, looking very closely.

His heart begins to pump faster and faster by the minute. Suddenly his room fell silent. As he stood staring into the reflection of the eyes in the mirror, the eyes stared back at him. The next thing you know, the reflection in the mirror suddenly screamed loud, shattering the mirror. His reflection jumped out from the mirror, with both arms stretched out. Then it began to choke Patrick.

With all he had, he tried to fight off, but the thang was too strong and has a death grip on his neck. His eyes rolled into the back of his head, exposing only the white of his eyes. The veins in the arms of his reflection, bulged as it attempts to choke the living life out of Patrick.

After a few seconds of being choked out, Patrick finally managed to break the grip of the reflection in the mirror sending him flying backwards, crashing into the wall behind him. He was so scared that he couldn't even move. It was like his body weighed two tons.

As Patrick rested against the wall for support, he felt the wall behind him move. Suddenly the wall formed arms, which began to wrap around his body like someone hugging him from behind. Then there were even more arms. Some grabbing at his legs and others pulled his arms. The arms protruding out the wall were covered with cuts. The fingernails were long and black. Most of the finger nails where broken. The boy tries to muster up the strength to fight to stay alive as his eyes grew bigger. He gasps for air, as the hands choke and cut off his air socket. Patrick was pinned up against the wall, as he continued to fight and kick. No matter how hard he tried to get away, he could not escape this wave of consternation.

The more he fought the more the fingernails pierced deep into his body. Blood poured from the boy's skin like water running. His t-shirt was shredded, hanging off his bleeding body.

Suddenly the middle of the floor begins to form a small crack right down the middle. Within the split of the floor was a bright red light that shine through. There was also a lite fog that raised from the crack in the floor. The room instantly became hotter. He started to sweat profusely.

The small crack slowly becomes bigger and bigger, then within a matter of minutes the crack becomes a large hole. The room is now filled with thick fog or it could have been smoke. The room was filled with a stench of a foul odor, which smelled like burning souls from hell. It was like hell had opened up. The smell was so strong and so bad that his eyes watered up.

He held his chest as he gasped for air like he was on his last breath. Flames protruded just beyond the boys' floor. By now, Patrick was sick to the stomach and can't take the foul odor any longer and he suddenly vomits all over himself uncontrollably. His stomach felt like he was jumping on a trampoline. He was sick as a dog. Blood begin to run from his nose rapidly.   There are no words to describe the evil horrible stench.

As he focuses on what's below, he witnessed the flames of hell shooting up through his floor. The howls of hell pierced his ears. The sounds of moans, screams and torture filled the room.

The burning toured souls begged for mercy. There were many yells and screams all at once. It sounded like a room full of people, all crying at the same time. The voices cried for mercy and for forgiveness, but it was far too late for their fate was already at hand.

Patrick could see the hands reaching up from the flames of the pits. The eyes of the souls in the pits where soulless, empty, with no names. Some had no eyes at all, and some lay motionless burnt to a total crisp.

Suddenly a voice announced in the hell hole.

"Welcome to your new home! " Patrick heard and understood clearly, the deep demoniac evil tone. Then a ferry of laughter erupted. The evil laughter bounced off the walls like a rubber ball. He saw an image of Bobby Berry appear through the fog.

In the corner, a swinging body hung by a rope from the ceiling of the room, the rope was attached to someone's neck. The cold bloody body swung back and forth, as it did it made a loud squeaking sound. Abruptly, the swinging body came to a stop. There was writing carved into the stomach that read, "Bobby lives and you die."

Just behind the hanging boy there was writing in blood on the wall that read in big bold letters. It said, "BOBBY MADE ME DO IT." The B's in Bobby were spilled backwards. The body had only a pair of boxers on and it was badly bruised.

Patrick's heart skipped two beats maybe even three. What is happening he thought to himself? This night must be a nightmare, he said to himself. But he only wished he was having a bad dream. Suddenly, as he stared at the boy hanging by the rope, its' head slowly raised up. Patrick's eyes grew with dismay and suspense. It was his own face.

Patrick begins to feel tightness around his own throat again. His tongue begins to protrude out of his mouth. It was if he were being choked himself again. His eyes start to roll backwards. He grabs his neck, grasping for air. He backed up against the wall looking in shock. He has seen his own self, dead hanging from the ceiling.

"No-no, this can't be," he says, in denial.

Then he begins to cry, but for him it was far too late. Suddenly he felt light headed like he was about to faint. Below the hanging body was a puddle of blood. It had formed from the blood dripping out of its mouth. Patrick felt so weak he struggled to stay on his feet. All the while the middle of his floor was still an open path way to hell full of burning souls and best believe Larry and Marcus faces were amongst the crowd.

Patrick took a quick glance back at his door and saw someone walked by. He noticed that his door was slightly open.

"Hey! Hey!" he yelled louder, "help me! Please help me!" he yelled once again.

No one responded. I got to get the hell out of here. He thought to himself. So, he attempted to get to his door by scaling along the edge of the wall. Trying to avoid falling in the huge hole that was forming in the middle of the floor. He tries not to look down, as he kicks at the burnt hands reaching out for him.

Breathing hard, scared and weak Patrick finally is at the open door to his freedom. He turned around to look back at the hell hole one more time, before he exited the room of horror.

Patrick placed one hand in the opening on the door. A cool breeze swept through, getting his attention. He turned back around towards the door, ready to pull himself out of the room of hell. A powerful rush of wind caused the twenty-pound steal door to close on Patrick's right hand. His fingers instantly detaches from the hand, sending his fingers flying in all different direction. Blood covered his shirt as he tucked the injured hand under his shirt. The boy screams loud enough to be heard for several blocks over. He is in excruciating pain. A pain beyond ones imagination.

Patrick struggled to his feet, too look out the window of the door. When he does, he sees Bobby Berry looking back at him with a slightly evil smile of his face. Just below Patrick is the devils pit of flames and there is no place for him to run or hide. Bobby suddenly appears on the other side of the door which is now the same side as Patrick was on.

Bobby eyes were a bright red and his skin was pale. He slowly walked over to Patrick. Patrick had never been this scared in his whole life. He was shaking like he was about to have a nervous breakdown. His teeth chattered together like he was freezing cold. Patrick wasn't sure what Bobby was going to do.

"You dead! No-no... you dead! You can't be alive," Patrick said, repeatedly in a frightened filled voice.

Bobby walked over to get closer to Patrick to say, "you can't kill me. Um already dead! Then suddenly he gave him a one hand shove to the chest. Both of his arms flew out, as if he was a bird about to take off for flight. Bobby smiled as he watched Patrick fall backwards into the demon pit of hell. His cries could be heard, as he falls until he disappeared into the eternal flames of hell.

CHAPTER 32

LADY IN THE SHOWER

Officer Johnson was on hall watch this particular night. He was sleeping in the dayroom on the couch as usual. He had been up for several minutes sweating heavily and his breathing was very rapid from a horrible dream he just had. As he woke up in a very state of fear, his eyes glanced across the dayroom then down B and C hall. It was quiet. Not a soul moving.

Damn. Um glad that was just a bad dream, he thought to himself. He grabbed his flash light and headed for the nearest closet to get some drying towels, but not before going to medical to check on Nurse Miller. For some reason this night the nurse seemed to be bothered by something. When the Officer asked what was wrong and why she was so quiet, she only replied that she was missing home. Officer Johnson consoled her and assured her that they would make it out alive.

The beautiful nurse smiled with an uneasy look in her pretty eyes. Then she said, "I hope so."

After that, he headed to the boys shower for a late night shower. Suddenly Officer Johnson remembered that it was something that he wanted to tell the nurse.

He turned around and went back to medical. As he opened the door with flash light in his hand, there was three bodies laid out on the floor completely covered in blood. Nurse Miller was one of the victims. She was laid out, face up. Officer Johnson's heart felt like it dropped down to his stomach.

"Please... please go get help. We need medical attention badly. We been shot. It was... it was the head nurse, nurse Young." the man's voice was weak, as he laid on the floor covered in blood, clutching his stomach.

Officer Johnson was filled with fear from head to toe. He felt like he couldn't get his body to move. When the officer made contact with the unknown man on the floor, he noticed his guts were hanging out his stomach. The officer ran as fast as he could to get some assistance. As he got back on the unit, he saw Officer Hill and Simms.

"Hurry! Hurry!" he said, with urgency to the two officer's busting through the door.

"Johnson what the hell wrong with you?" said Officer Hill.

The two officer's exchange looks. "Man just come with me quick."

Officer Johnson ran out the unit door heading back to medical as fast as he could, almost tripping over his own feet. The other two officers were right behind him.

"What's going on Johnson?" Officer Simms asked, following close behind. He didn't respond.

"We got to help these people!" Officer Johnson said, as he yanked the door open to medical. When he opened the door the room was clear. The room was empty. No one was present.

"Johnson! What the fuck is going on man?" Officer Hill called from behind gasping for air.

"Nurse Miller! Nurse Miller!" Officer Johnson called aloud, looking around the empty room.

"Nurse Miller! Man, what the fuck you talking bout," said Officer Simms.

"Man, I promise I was just talking to her five minutes ago!"

"Johnson have you lost yo damn mind? Nurse Miller got killed over 30 years ago. Man what hell is wrong with you!"

A third degree of fright came over him. Officer Johnson had no words, nor could he explain seeing and talking to the nurse. Later that night he did everything he could to get those images out of his head. He tried to sleep, but he couldn't close his eyes, the thoughts of the nurse and the dead bodies came rushing back. So he thought a shower would relax him. When he got in the shower area, he noticed something out of place. He saw that the shower door was unlocked.   Strange he thought to himself. Something just didn't look and feel right, because he knew that the shower was locked before.

He had been doing security rounds every two hours or so, and the last security rounds he did was just before he had fell asleep. The shower door was locked, but maybe someone came on the unit while I was sleeping and unlocked it he thought. So with that, he didn't make much of it. He proceeded to the shower. When he walked in he heard the shower water already running. There was also a very dim light coming from the area. The other shower stalls were dark.

As he slowly approached the shower where the water was running, he noticed someone standing in the shower. It looked like a woman. A very pretty woman. It felt like he had falling into one of those good dreams. He had no idea who this person was or what she was doing in the shower. As a matter of fact, he pinched himself a few times just to make sure he wasn't dreaming. Damn. He thought, to himself, as he looked at this mysterious lady from behind with lust in his eyes and bad intentions in his heart.

It appeared to be a white female. He couldn't see her face, but from behind she looked to have a body of a 25-year-old. She had a thin built, and about 5'6" with long beautiful blond hair.

Officer Johnson begins to quickly remove his utility belt right down to his boxers, as he moved closer to the unknown lady. As he joined her, he begins to rub and caress her body as he stood behind her. Suddenly the officer noticed something strange about the lady. He noticed that this lady's skin began to feel rough as he rubbed her. Very rough in fact. Her skin wasn't soft like at first, no not at all. Instead, her skin was rough and hard almost like fish skills.

"What- the- fuck!" Officer Johnson said, with a frown on his face looking frighten and surprised at the same time. He then took two steps back. As he did, the unknown lady turned around now facing him. Now, he could see the mysterious lady's face. The face was rotten. Worms slowly swarmed in and out one of her eye sockets. The lower part of her jaw bone was gone. It looked as if she had been buried for months, then dug back up. She smelled like a skunk. She stunk like hell.

With his eyes wide open, his mouth dropped to the floor. He took another step back in shock and disbelief. As he stepped back, the decaying face lady stepped forward with both her arms stretched out reaching for him.

"Come to me, oh baby come to me," said the lady. Then the lady began to speak in a high pitch squeaking voice, repeating again, "come to me, come to me." She begins to laugh exposing her top row of rotten teeth. A great deal of her hair was missing in the front of her head. The lower side of her face was exposing her bones. As he focused on that area of her face he could see maggots and bugs crawling inside of her face. His heart was beating uncontrollably.

"No!" he yelled. "No!" he yelled again, but this time much louder. He moved back away from the hideous lady. As he attempted to move out the way, he suddenly backs into the back wall of the shower. He frantically turns to the door and begins to pull on the handle trying to exit the shower. As he pulls on the door it seem to be locked. The decaying face lady is getting closer and closer to him. Close enough to reach out and touch him. Too close for comfort. The dim light suddenly goes out. Now it is completely dark, so dark you can't see your own hand in front of your face. Then the room gets quiet. The only thing that can be heard is the officer's heavy breathing and the water dripping.

He is breathing heavy in and out. Next thing you know, his eyes peer deep into the darkness of the shower. His hand still wrapped tight around the handle of the shower door.

"Hey!" Officer Johnson yells out into the darkness of the room, but there is no answer. "Hey!" he yells again this time pulling on the door even harder. Then the face of the decaying woman reappears only inches away from his face.

She was close enough to kiss him. He screamed as he fell through the opening shower door. He quickly stood to his feet, closed the door and then locked it. For a moment, the alarmed officer peered at the lady through the shower window. The lady's long blond hair blew all about, as if someone had turned on a high powered fan. She began to bang on the door hard enough, that it seemed like she would break it down, as she pled to the officer to open the door. The lady's mouth moved, but no words could be heard on the other side of the plexiglass window.

As the officer turns to run away from the shower, he turns to look back. It was like the lady was moving in slow motion, yelling for him and still banging on the window. He ran to the dayroom and sat down in a state of shock.

It's been some days since the shower incident and things seemed to get stranger. Tony has been telling him that his radio has been playing without batteries. He also told Officer Johnson that he has heard all kind of voices coming from the radio.

"One night," Tony said, he was awakened by the radio. "It was playing that scary chant; you can't kill me."

Of course this did not surprise him at all. As Officer Johnson thoughts lead him down a mental journey of the unexplained, he suddenly remembered something. "Damn! I almost forgot to do that." Officer Johnson's says, as he springs up from the couch in the day room. He stretches his arm out, as if he was reaching for the ceiling; followed by a big yawn. Then he begins to make his way, to the kitchen to retrieve some snacks he promised to give to a few residents. As he enters the kitchen, it is very quiet and cold. The area is well lit, from the daylight shining through the kitchen windows. He rubs his hands together, trying to generate some heat. This is oddly noticeable to him because, throughout the rest of the building it is hot. When he reaches out to open the door of the walk in refrigerator, which was not working. It was used it to store nonperishable items. All of a sudden, he hears the sounds of movement and a lot of commotion coming from behind him. He stops what he is doing and listens. Out of nowhere, people are running in a panic his direction.

"Run! Run! He's coming," one person roared, as they passed.

"He's got a gun!" someone else screamed, as they ran passed. They had the facial expressions of pure terror. It appeared to be a group of 10 people, running for their lives. It seemed as though, they were all running from something, and looking for the emergency exit.

Then suddenly, someone yelled, "motherfuckers!" Followed by a gun shot. The gun shot sounded like a big massive explosion. The shooter was not visible from Officer Johnson's position. Four people dropped instantly. Blood splattered against the walls. Their bodies were riddled with buckshot's. As Officer Johnson realized what was happening, right in front of his eyes, sweat begins to cover his face. His pulse and heart begin to flutter uncontrollably. He attempts to run for his life with the others, but he can't move, nor can he feel his legs. He is suddenly paralyzed with horror. Just a few feet away, he hears the gunman yelling a flurry of curse words. He also hears the shooter reloading his shotgun. He can feel the gunman getting closer and closer. He suddenly opens his eyes from this horrible nightmare. When he awakes, the sinister nurse is standing only inches away from him. He has a loaded shotgun pointed right at Officer Johnson's forehead. He realized this was no dream. Again, his heart raced rapidly. Sweat poured like water from his forehead. The officer didn't know what to do. The sinister nurse stood behind the long shot gun, with the most insane look ever. His eyes looked into Officer Johnson eyes. One eye was slightly cocked to the left, he looked totally insane. In his eyes, it appeared his soul was absent. His mind was in a fixed position of mass murder. The deranged nurse was nurse Young. He displayed an evil smile, exposing his grimy, gritty rotten teeth. Then without warning, he pulled the trigger. The shot gun exploded and sounded like a bomb. The sound ricocheted off the walls, hard enough to break the windows. Officer Johnson brains blew out the back of his head. His brains and fragments from his skull splattered all over the couch, floor and walls.

"No! No! Ah!" Officer Johnson yells out loud, rolling off the couch. He crashes hard onto the floor, as he continued to kick and scream.

"No! No! No!" he says, shaking his head and still kicking, as he realizes he had a nightmare within a nightmare.

To him, it all seems to be, way too real. As he lay there on the floor, still breathing heavily, he checks himself. He feels his head, it was all intact. He wanted to make sure he was in a state of reality and not in another nightmare. When he finally clears his head, he sees he is in the dayroom alone. He gathers his thoughts and gets up off the floor. He heads to an empty room to wash up. When he enters the empty cell, something unexpectedly catches his attention. As he passed the toilet, he notices blood inside. After he saw the blood, he thought back on the time when Tony told him he had blood in his toilet or maybe it was his sink. When he looked at the toilet, he saw something else really strange. As he steered down into the commode he could see the blood bubbling. It appeared to be boiling.

"What the hell?" he thought to himself.

He noticed something moving around slowly in the toilet. He took a step back. He has a confused expression on his face. Suddenly the toilet flushed on its own. It made a loud evil sound. The blood began to overflow, as if the toilet was stopped up. He slowly and cautiously moved close to the overflowing toilet. Then he moved closer to the toilet, and then he moved even closer. All of a sudden Bobby Berry comes out of the blood filled toilet, grabbing him before he even knew what hit him, pulling him into the toilet. On the way down, Officer Johnson grabs the rim of the toilet with both hands. He was trying to stop the flow of the flush. He held on for dear life. His face is completely covered with blood, expressing the look of a terrified man. His eyes quickly shift back and forth, as he yelled as loud as he could for help. The doomed officer fights for his life, as blood splashes all over the bathroom. Suddenly Officer Johnson disappears into the murky blood filled toilet. For a moment, the movement stops and the room falls silent. All of a sudden, Officer Johnson's arms emerge out of the toilet. It was as if he was making, one last effort to save himself. Then he was yanked under the blood, disappearing for good. Bubbles float to the top.

CHAPTER 33

THE CLEANSING

By the end of February, the snow begins to show signs of melting. The face of the sun was bright and present again. Without a doubt the facility had gone through its fair share of catastrophic events. And the place will never be the same again. But now, it was time for a new start. As the snow subsides, Georgia power was called out to restore all the lost power issues and like magic within a couple of days the power was on again. The building had not only taking a beating inside but, outside as well.

While the facility was undergoing a major over haul, Officer Simms, and Hill left never to return. Maybe the drama was just too much for them to handle. While the others walked away, Officer Parker elected to stay. The county had some other officer's from neighboring facilities to assist during the rebuilding process. It was later found out that the director, Mr. Boykin was found dead frozen in his car. It appeared that he ran into a ditch, while he was attempting to come to the facility. He was probably trying to come to render aid to the security staff.

In the meanwhile, Officer Parker's main concern was ridding the building of all evil spirits. He was convinced that this was something that just had to happen before any peace could come about. So, he made the decision to reach out to a local priest to help him in this time of need. The man for the job was no other than Priest Moultrie and he was more than delighted to answer the call.

Once the facility was back up and running Priest Moultrie paid the building a visit. The night Priest Moultrie came was gloomy- gloomy indeed. The priest was draped in an all-black robe with white trimming.

The priest's robe was long almost touching the floor. The man held a bible in his right hand and a small black leather bag in the other hand. The priest was an old white man looked to be in his early seventies. He was gray headed and clean cut. The priest had been performing exorcisms for the past twenty years, so needless to say he wasn't new to this.

When the priest arrived to the center, he was met by Officer Parker. All the residents were on lock down due to the father's visit. Officer Parker informed him of all that he knew about what happened the months before. All he knew was five people had been killed and there was an evil presence. He didn't know any specific information. Once the father got the information, he went straight to work.

"This place has a very dark evil presence," Father Moultrie said, in a low tone as he and Officer Parker entered the unit together, "the spirit is strong my friend, very strong," he added. Then suddenly, he stopped in his tracks and turned to the officer and said, "and it doesn't want me here."

Officer Parker was already reluctant to do this, but he knew it had to be done. As Father Moultrie walked about the dayroom, he began to pray in a low tone, as he did the room temperature changed and the windows begin to shake violently.

The lights in the dayroom begin to flicker off and on like that of a strobe light. It became so hot that both men started to sweat. The priest's eye glasses began to fog up, but Father Moultrie was unmoved by the evil antics

"Hold this for me, please," The priest said, handing the officer his small leather bag, and then he wiped the fog from his glasses. The television came on in full blast, but only for a moment. The officer took cover jumping behind the brave priest.

The priest asked the officer to reach in his black bag and pull out the small bottle with the water in it. As the father walked down the halls, he began to splash water on the walls. The walls sizzle like bacon in a frying pan. Then traces of smoke followed. The two men looked at one another with amazement.

When the two men approached B unit, the evil seem to awaken even more. The locked room doors begin to fly open and shut repeatedly; as it did a gust of wind blew through out the unit, almost blowing off the priest glasses.

"I bind you demon!" the priest says as he adjust his glasses. Then he reached over to Officer Parker, whom was by this time shaking in his shoes. The priest went into his bag and pulled out is holy water. He begins to pray louder, as he did he sprayed the holy water on the walls.

As the water hit the walls of the unit, a deep demoniac voice called out, "no-no, it burns!"

The sounds coming from the walls sounded like someone was in excruciating pain. As the priest continued to splash water on the walls, the walls begin to open up, as if a knife or razor had cut the flesh of a human. Blood flowed heavily, dripping down the walls unto the floor.

"Ah- you murderer of the flesh and spirit," the demoniac voice boldly denounced as the smoke from the cuts, float to the ceiling. Without warning Officer Parker yells and scream, and runs out of the hall. He headed to the dayroom, leaving the priest all alone, but without fear the priest continued his mission.

"In the name of the Holy Father, free this place of the evil presence!" the priest said, in a loud tone with his right hand balled into a fist.

"You are the flesh of my bones, our heart beat as one you motherfucker, I curse you. I curse you, you bastard," an evil voice called out of nowhere.

Father Moultrie walked over to C unit, as he did he looked into the first room to his right. He saw a man standing in the window with the face of a goat with long horns. The eyes of the goat head was two different colors, the right eye was white and the other eye was bright red.

When the Father Moultrie focused his attention back down the hall way he noticed that the floor on C unit had turned into a pool of blood. The blood covered up to the priests' ankles. He reached inside his shirt and pulled out his neckless that had a cross on it. As he continued to pray, walking down the hall, up from the pool of blood appeared to be a person. The priest paused for a moment to see what was ahead of him. He noticed as he looked, it was an old white woman with long stringy blonde hair, rising out of the shadow of the pool of blood. The old lady was wearing what appeared to be a gown, but it was hard to tell because she was covered in blood from head to toe. The old lady stood there in the middle of the hall, staring back at the priest with blood dripping from her body.

"I bind you back to the gates of hell," the father said, as he sprayed his holy water on the blood covered old lady. As the holy water hit the old lady, her skin opened like she was being sliced by a machete knife. The old lady yelled like a howling wolf. Smoke came from her arms, where she had been hit with the holy water.

"Leave this place. You are not welcomed here," the old lady said, with both her arms stretched out slowly walking toward the priest. Then suddenly the priest raised his bible and pointed it in her direction. Then he yelled something that could not be understood. The old lady's head cocked upward like she was looking up at the ceiling.

"Ooh, put that away!" the lady said, as if she was hurting badly. The old lady takes two more steps backwards, then falls into the pool of blood disappearing.

Suddenly Officer Parker and another officer ran down to help the Father. Once he was on the hall, he began to stare into the darkness of the room, as if he had seen something inside, but nothing was present. Then out of the blue, the ventriloquist puppet: Mr. Michael pops up in the window of the door like a Jack in the box, with a big crash. Both the men were caught off guard, and they almost jumped out of their skin, except the priest. When they looked back again, the window was clear. No one was standing there. The officers and the priest continued down D unit hallway. As they passed the doors, the sounds of terror were heard coming from the rooms. Spirits of all kinds stood in the window of the rooms watching the men as they walked by.

"Help... please help us!" they all cried out to the father.   Some of their faces were pasted to the windows. Some were banging on the doors.

As Father Moultrie and the men past one room there was a very bright light coming from this particular room. The men stopped and looked inside. The room was clean and everything in the room was white as snow. The walls of the room were padded. Inside there, stood a man unrobed who looked like he had been badly beaten. From the ceiling of the room, hung a household extension cord. The badly beaten man stood on a chair and placed the extension cord around his neck.

"No!" the father said, as he tried to open the door to save the man. The door was locked. The man looked at Father Moultrie with empty eyes, then he jumped off the wooden chair he was standing on. As the rope tighten from his weight, his neck snapped in two like a tooth pick. Blood poured from the man's nose and vomit spilled out of his mouth. His body dangled and swung from one side to the other. The priest and the two officers turned their heads. The priest then took out the cross neckless he was wearing around his neck and kissed it.

He and the two officers slowly walked down to the room next to Tony's room. The door suddenly flew open crashing hard against the wall. Glass shattered all over the floor. Father Moultrie walked with the officers, as they followed with caution behind him.

Inside the room was a boy, he appeared to be sleeping. This boy's name was Jarret Blackman. He was a white male and 15 years of age. He was a good kid that never gave the officers any problems. He was locked up for theft by receiving. This was his first time ever being locked up.

The priest and the two officers approached the sleeping boy. The room was silent. Father Moultrie walked over to the bed where the boy was laying. The two officers were standing in the door way. They were close to one another. They were almost huddled together. They didn't know what to expect. The priest orders both men to stay close by.

"Please- look under the bed," Father Moultrie said looking at one of the officer's. The officer slowly bends down on his hands and knees. He got on the floor and looked under the bed.

"What the hell? Hey Parker, there is a doll under here!" the officer said looking back at the Priest.

"Don't touch that doll!" Officer Parker yelled out, to the unbeknown officer. "Don't worry it's just a dang doll," the officer replied, while reaching under the bed with one arm, as he was looking back at Officer Parker.

The officer reached for the doll, then all the sudden and without warning the doll jumped and screamed loudly. It was as if the doll had suddenly came alive. Then the doll grabs the officer by the arm and begins to try and pull the officer under the bed. The officer quickly snatches away, as he moved back from the bed.

"What the hell!" the scared officer said, "there's something under the bed."

When Officer Parker checked under the bed, he did not see anything except Jarret's shoes.

"This room... the evil presence is here. I can feel it breathing, staring at me," the priest whispered. Then he took out his prayer oil, tapped some on his right index finger and begins to rub some on the boy's forehead as he prayed.

As the priest put the oil on the sleeping boy's forehead, it started to bubble up like a pot of hot boiling water. The boy's eyes were suddenly wide open. His eyeballs were as black as a witch's cat. The priest stops immediately and orders the two officers to hand cuff the boy to his bed.

The officer's walked over to the boy almost like they were tip toeing, because they didn't won't to wake him. They did just as the priest requested and cuffed the boy to his bed. To be safe the officers also place shackles on his legs.

Once the boy was hand cuffed, Father Moultrie begin to speak to the boy saying, "come out- come out and speak to me."

The boy's eyes were filled with darkness. He started to release an evil chuckle. The priest drew closer to put more oil on the boy's head. The boy begins to move his head to avoid such contact of the healing oil.

"Keep that away from me," the demoniac spirit inside the boy demanded in a calm tone. His voice was deep, and spoke very proper.

Father Moultrie begins to pray once again, as he did the boy scratched the metal post on his bed rail. It was the sound like someone scratching a chalk board at school. You know that sound that just made your skin crawl. His finger nail was long and discolored. As he continued to scratch the side of the metal bed rail, his finger cracked, then begins to fold back before the nail finally broke down into his skin.

"What have you come for?" the demon asked speaking through the boy.

"I come too free this place of you and your evil spirits," the priest replied looking over the boy from head to toe. Then the boy started to yank on the hand cuffs as if he was trying to break away from the hands and legs irons.

As the boy sees Father Moultrie reach for his cross and the holly water, the boy begin to cry out loud to the top of his voice, "what's that? What are you doing? No! No! Don't touch me with that that!"

As the holy water hits the boy, his skin sizzles which sound like bacon in a frying pan. "You bastard!" the boy said. Then the sheets flew off his bed, as if someone had yanked them away falling directly behind the men. The possessed boy begins to shake violently, so hard that his whole bed seemed like it was going to break. Then miraculously even with the hand cuffs on, the boy managed to sit up in his bed. Then without warning the boy begins to throw up all over himself. Thick green slime slowly dripped down his mouth onto his shirt.

By now, the boy eyes had become green as grass and his skin was discolored. His lips were a dark blue. As the men peered at the boy, something appeared to be crawling under his skin. It came from his neck area; a huge cock roach came crawling out of his left eye.

With vomit all about his mouth, he begins to break out in laughter looking at Father Moultrie, "you think you can control me, but I control you."

Then the demon boy slowly laid back in his bed. The priest begins to pray even harder. As he does, the demon begins to mock every word the priest was saying. The Father paused for a moment, then reached in his bag and pulls out the cross and places it on the boy chest.

Suddenly, a gust of wind sweeps through the room. The toilet also begins to flush repeatedly. The doors begin to open and close on its own.

"Release the soul of this child now devil. I command you, lose him," the priest yells, leaning over the possessed boy.

Then, the demoniac boy begins to talk in voices, which sound to be like a record being played backwards. The next thing you know, the boy's hands begin to bend backwards at the wrist looking like his hand would snap at any moment.

As Father Moultrie continued to denounce the devil, the boy begins to rise from his bed snapping off the hand cuffs and leg irons, like it was a cheap toy. The boy was floating in midair. The hand cuffs and leg irons dangled from his hands and feet.

The two officers looked in total disbelief and fear. The wall next to the bed begin to sound and move just like a human heart beat. It was like the wall was alive itself. As the boy floated, he took his right hand and slowly scratched the wall. The wall peeled like wall paper, but underneath it looked like the inside of a human body and was covered with a multitude of maggot's crawling all about. The room's stench was that of death ten times over. The officers held their mouths as to keep from throwing up all over the place. The walls became hot to the touch. The demon boy laughs once more. It was too much for the officers to bare. They both ran out the room returning to the dayroom.

As the priest kept praying, the sound of a child's voice is heard through the prayers. Then the boy suddenly drops out of the air, crashing hard on to the mattress. The young boy begins to cry uncontrollably.

Father Moultrie quickly places his bible back into his black bag. Then, he leans over and hold the boy in his arms. With tears in his eyes, he looked up at the priest and asked, "what happened?"

As the he rubbed the boy's head, he simply replied, "you have just been freed my son... you have just been freed." The priest looked towards the heavens with praise.

CHAPTER 34

EIGHT MONTHS LATER

It's been five months, since the worst storm in Georgia history hit and only one month since the priest: Father Moultrie rid the facility of all its evil spirits. Since then a lot of things have changed and of course the snow and ice is finally gone. All the staff with the exception of Officer Parker has left. He is the only one who remained. Everyone else are new recruits from neighboring states and they have no clue of the events that took place just months before.

By the way, Officer Parker has been promoted. He is a lieutenant now. As far as the others officers it was discovered that, Officer Simms is now working as a counselor with the state, and Officer Hill is working with Atlanta City Sheriff's Office as a Deputy Sheriff.

It was said that Ms. Berry, Bobby's mother was successful in holding the county liable for her son's death. The amount awarded from the law suit, was never disclosed. No amount of money could never replace the loving son she lost. Her faith in God was the only thing that she leaned on for life and strength.

As far as the residents, most of them were shipped to different facilities in different counties to settle their legal issues due to the dramatic events that took place the months before. All that is left are the stories of how the things went bump in the middle of the night and how four residents and one crooked officer was masterly killed one by one. And how one boy killed another boy and got away with it.

To most of the new kids and staff, all that they say happened is only another dumb trumped up story; like some kind of urban legend. Maybe, because the staff and residents had to be there, so maybe it made it easier for residents to do their time and staff to earn an honest living without being scared. Maybe that was the best way deal with it and to think of it, as just another crazy story.

After several months of peace, things are once again back to normal. It's as though the worst of times are well over, for this facility. As far as Tony goes, he is of course is back to his old tricks, you know, taking people food, bulling and of course giving the security staff a hard time with the exception of the new Lieutenant. (LT. Parker)

Although Tony is behaving badly, he is also very happy, because in a matter of days he will be a free young man. His release date is closely approaching.

So with that fact, Tony feels that he can say and do what whatever he wants. He feels like he doesn't have to listen to anybody. Here lately, all he has been doing is walking around talking about fuck this and fuck that, um getting out in two days. And this is all day and all night.

The staff can't wait for this boy to leave. He has been their worst nightmare come true. So, needless to say, they are just as ready for him to leave just as much as he is.

The truth of the matter is, that he is happy just to have survived this crazy situation. He has seen and heard a lot of things. Three of his buddies have been killed and his friend Officer Johnson was killed also. He has also killed someone while being in here.

Tony is happy that Father Moultrie rid the place of all the evil spirits and that Bobby Berry didn't come back to kill him like he did everyone else. Over all he was just happy to have survived and have a chance for a brand new beginning.

For him this was not just another day, in fact it's a very special day. It's his last day of being locked up, and tomorrow he will be leaving. He will be a free man, putting all this behind him forever. So, never the less Tony is a happy person right now.

On this day, Tony was up first thing in the morning, with a big smile on his face and tells the officer thank you as they let him out his room. This of course shocks the officers because these kinds of words don't ever come out of his mouth. Thank you wasn't even a part of his vocabulary.

"Your welcome," the officer replied in an uncertain voice, as if the officer was thinking what's next?

Tony tells the officer, he had been locked for a year and a half and he didn't want any trouble. He was just ready to go home.

Then, he added that he was not going to give nobody any problems. Again, the officers were taking a back by his unusual mannerisms.

"Well okay, we would appreciate that," said one officer.

Just as Tony promised, he got in line placed his hands behind his back without being told. Everyone was looking dumb founded by his super polite positive behavior. Even the other residents were shocked.

The group of boys all was counted. The count was called in to central control via radio and then the group of boys was escorted into the dining area.

The group sat quietly and ate their breakfast. After breakfast, there was a church program that followed. When Lt. Parker asked, who wanted to stay for church, everyone was shocked when Tony raised his hand quietly indicating that he wanted to attend. Again they couldn't believe it.

At this point, the staff was really beginning to get a little worried and concerned, to say the least. I mean, all the time he has been locked up, the only thing Tony ever did was cuss, fuss and raise hell. Then all the sudden, he wants to act like an angel. It's safe to say, the staff felt better when Tony was acting a fool and behaving like an animal. He was trying to act all good and at this point the staff didn't know what he was up to, acting this way.

Tony did attend church on this morning and things went well. Tony even seemed to have a genuine interest in the church program. After church, the residents all went back to the unit for recreation then lunch. All the while, Tony was on his best behavior, something that the staff has never seen before.

On this day, all Tony talked about was going home and getting back in school and have good clean fun. He proclaimed to be a changed man. He seemed to have made a complete change almost overnight; or has he. I mean think about it, all this time he been raising hell. Something just didn't seem right about all this so called good behavior. There were even some events were Tony swiftly corrected some of the boys for cursing and disrespecting the officers. All the officers could say was, wow!

All the officers knew that anything could happen, at any time with a person like Tony. They were not convinced by this so called new change. They felt that not one minute that he was being genuine. So, even though he seems to be on his best behavior, they knew he hasn't left the building yet. They couldn't be at ease until Tony was locked in his room and was out the building. The staff couldn't wait for the morning, because that they all knew he would be leaving to go home first thing in the morning. So, of course they were ready to party once he is finally out.

Later that night at 8:00 pm, it was time for the white cards to go to bed. One of the officers stepped in front of the television and paused the movie. He cut on the dayroom lights and announced that it was time for all the white cards to go to bed.

Every officer's eye was on Tony, because they were just waiting to see what he was going to do when it was time for to go to bed. Tony along with about 9 other white cards slowly got up together and gathered their things. They begin to make their way down the halls to go to their rooms for the night.

"Alright, y'all boys be easy. Y'all know um out tomorrow morning," Tony said, walking slowly to his door as he looked over his shoulder.

There was one officer standing at the end of each hall way, to ensure that the boys go to their rooms as they were instructed. The officer on D hall watched Tony like a hawk, as he calmly walked down the hall to his room. As he got closer to his room, the officer felt like the world was moving in slow motion. Tony slowly reached out his right hand to open his cell door. Then suddenly, he ran down the hall yelling, "fuck that shit um going home tomorrow."

He sung aloud running up and down the hall, flipping things over as he did with a playful evil smile on his face.

Tony ran into the dayroom and continued to dance and buck screaming all kind of obscenities, " I fooled y'all asses. Fuck y'all um bucking! Y'all fuck niggas gone have to get it with your muscle."

Then he begins to sing that song that all the juveniles like to sing, which was "get with yo muscle," he repeated over and over again and again.

Then, the others begin to join in on the chant. The next thing you know, everyone in the dayroom was singing that ridiculous song and banging on their doors. He had the whole unit in an up roar. The officer begins to lock the whole dayroom down, because Tony refused to lock down.

Now, Tony is running all around the dayroom pushing furniture over and being a real pain in the butt, "hey why are you acting this way Tony?" one officer called out.

"Because I don't give a fuck, and um going home tomorrow," he replied still carrying on like a fool. Then he paused a moment, as an officer walks up on him like he was going to grab Tony.

"You betta not touch me. Um gone swing on you, if you put yo fucking hands on me," he says, as if he was starting to tire out, "um serious, y'all fuck niggas bat not touch me."

"Tony stop! I need you to go to your room," said the officer standing near him.

"I need you to get some muthafuckin Tic Tac's. Yo shit get me on lean," Tony says, being rude.

"Tony! I need you to get to your room!" Lt. Parker insisted.

By now, all the officers have surrounded him, trying to catch him, so they can put him into his room. The bad boy continues to disobey and disrespect the staff.

"Um going to ask you one more time- go to your room, boy!" the lieutenant demanded.

"Fuck you!" he said, looking straight into the officer's eyes, with that slight evil smile on his face.

"I ain't going nowhere," he added with his arms folded, then he begins to square off with the security staff.

"The hell with all this shit! Go get that damn camera," Lt. Parker demanded. Suddenly, Tony took off his gray t-shirt, smiling like something was funny.

"Oh shit! It's on now nigga," the boy said, with his fist balled up tightly.

Another officer walks over to the control room window to retrieve the camera and return to the defiant resident. The officer's address Tony yet again, looking at the camera stating the boy's behavior and that he has been asked several times to go too his room, but he has refused all directives. Then, while the camera was recording he was asked two more times, but he would not comply.

After the last command for him to go inside his room, all three officer's bomb rushed him all the sudden at the same time. But the thing was, Tony wasn't even trying to fight. He wasn't even really mad at all. He just wanted to wrestle with the officers. Of course, the officers were in no mood to play around with him, they were very upset with his negative behavior.

After about three to four minutes of him kicking and wrestling, the security staff finally gain control of the boy. I mean he put up a fight, but his fight just wasn't enough for the three strong officers'. Once they gained control of Tony, two of the officers had him by his arms. By the time it was over, he was flat out of breath and was bending over gasping for air. Lt. Parker held the camera recording the incident.

"Y'all still lame motherfuckers. Um going home tomorrow," he cursed, screamed and yelled all the way down from the dayroom to his room.

He said, "um getting out tomorrow!" he continued to shout repeatedly over and over.

As the two officer's secured both of his hands from moving, they escorted him to his room. Just as they turned the key to open Tony's door. He takes a step into his and something viciously attacks him.

Suddenly, there are very loud screams. There is also a lot of commotion. It's as if the camera is being shaken and being thrown all about. Then suddenly, the face of Bobby Berry appears in the view of the camera. But only seconds at a time. His eyes where big, white and piercing. His anger expression exposed his razor sharp teeth. Then in only in a matter of seconds, the walls of the small room are completely covered with Tony's blood and guts. His blood splats against the lens of the camera. The camera falls crashing hard to the floor, while still recording showing just a portion of Tony's face with his head was bleeding profusely. His right eye had been gauged clean out the socket and his head was twisted backward from the body. Dead. Then the whole room goes black.

CHAPTER 35

10 YEARS LATER

It's been ten long years since the horrible death of young Bobby Berry. To this day, rumors still swirl in the air about what really happened to him. There is an even bigger mystery about what happen to Officer Johnson, Tony and his crew. By the way, the film footage of the death of Tony, which was caught on tape was never found.

There has also been a major shift in the staff and the residents. Lt. Parker has been retired for five years now. The majority of the staff and residents are white. The whole atmosphere is totally different. Things are now a lot calmer and laid back. The place is more like a community summer camp, then a detention center.

"Okay everyone it is now bed time. Listen, you guys had a great day today. Thank you all for being on your best behavior," the officer's say to the residents, as they start to shuffle to their rooms for bed time.

"Hey y'all remember," one resident say's aloud with a mischievous smile on his face standing in the middle of the dayroom.

"This is Sunday, August 29. You all know that mean."

"Yeah, it's the ten-year anniversary of Bobby Berry's death," another answered.

"Do you think he'll be back tonight?"

"Yeah right," one boy say's.

The group all share a laugh as they continue to their rooms for the night.

"That story isn't true.   It's just a stupid urban legend... I can't believe you all believe that," one boy responds.

"Attention.   Attention!" a lady's voice announced over the loud speaker.

"It is now count time in the facility."

By now, all the residents are locked down in the rooms and the staff is ready to do their nightly head count. Three officers count each hall B, C, and D. Then they compare the numbers in the dayroom.

"I have 22 on B hall," one the officer announced. All the officers agreed.

"I have 8 on C unit," one said. The other officers looked puzzled, and then the other two officers confirmed that they both had count only seven on C unit.

"Well, I counted 8," the officer said with confidence.

"That can't be right, C unit has been 7 all day long."

"Okay, no big deal," said the officer, "I may have miscounted. What did y'all get on D unit?"

"I got 24 on D hall," and all agreed on the D hall count.

"We'll, let's just recount C unit one more time."

All three officers walked down to C unit and begin to check and count each door after each other. Then they got to door C-06, there was a mysterious boy standing with his back towards the door.

"Okay he makes 8 on this unit," one officer say's to the other officers, as they all have a laugh.

"Hey!" the officer calls out to the mysterious boy standing in the window.

"Hey!" the officer calls out again, this time knocking on the window to get the boys' attention.

"What's your name kid?"

The boy slowly turned around facing the window and says, "Bobby Berry."

The End